.97

Fisher, Alan
The rage of angels

THE
RAGE
of
ANGELS

THE
RAGE
of
ANGELS

Alan Fisher

CARROLL & GRAF PUBLISHERS, INC.
NEW YORK

First Carroll & Graf edition 1997

Carroll & Graf Publishers, Inc.
260 Fifth Avenue
New York, NY 10001

Library of Congress Cataloging-in-Publication Data

Fisher, Alan (Alan E.)
      The rage of angels / Alan Fisher. — 1st Carroll & Graf ed.
          p.   cm.
      ISBN 0-7867-0409-8 (cloth)
      1. World War, 1914-1918—Aerial operations, British—Fiction.
   2. World War, 1914-1918—Campaigns—France—Fiction.   I. Title.
   PR6056.I773R34   1997
   823' .914—dc21   96-53910
                                                                               CIP

Manufactured in the United States of America

For Ernest Fredrick Fisher
Private No. 202921, East Surrey Regiment,
who at eighteen fought through some of
the great battles of the First World War.
And for his wife, Minnie Esther.

One

THE DAY had begun.

The blunt-nosed machines were grey in the early morning light, and there was moisture on the rigging wires and canvas surfaces. The air was still. Marten Corby frowned at the sky as he pulled on his leather helmet and goggles, then he swung himself up into the open cockpit. Duncan stood watching, his stubby hands on the hips of his dirty overalls.

Donovan was last as usual, squeezing his huge frame into the cockpit of his machine, while Peter's Hispano engine fired, caught, spat unevenly for a moment, then settled down to a steady roar, shattering the stillness of the morning.

Marten checked to see if all the control surfaces worked, then switched the fuel on. Duncan wound the propeller to find compression. What an ungodly hour to cross the front. Nobody should get killed this early in the day, it wasn't decent. He set the throttle, flicked on the magneto switch and gave Duncan the thumbs-up sign. Duncan swung the propeller and the engine burst into life, flames jetting from the stub exhausts and casting an orange glow in the half-light. The tachometer needle swung then steadied. He watched the oil pressure building up as he fastened his safety belt.

Peter and Drinkwater were already taking off, and Killer Smith's machine was moving slowly forward. Marten followed, peering along the side of the fuselage as the SE5 wobbled over the cinder apron and onto the field. There wasn't much ground mist. He could see the trees at the field's end, and the square church tower of St Eduarde and just beyond that the sugar beet factory.

He pressed himself hard against the back of the seat and eased open the throttle. The flickering arc of the propeller blurred as the engine thundered and the machine surged forward, bumping and juddering over the uneven surface of the field towards the church tower. The tail came up, and the pounding vibration ceased as the wheels lifted. And he was over the sugar beet factory, hauling up the right wings for a fast, climbing turn. That should wake the village. The mayor would probably complain again.

The heady sensation of speed eased as the village diminished in the thin m' below him. He spiralled up steadily and slotted in the left side of Peter. With a bit of luck the Huns wouldn't be about this early.

Killer Smith was flying with his left hand and pulling his red silk scarf over his mouth with his right. His SE5 was a little too close to Peter's, as though he were unconsciously jockeying with Peter for the lead. Donovan was at the rear of the echelon, flying slightly above, out of the slipstream from the other propellers, and his machine was swinging very slightly from side to side in a steady, rhythmical motion. He was probably singing one of those interminable Irish ballads.

They hadn't reached three thousand feet, but already Marten could feel the cold eating into him. He glanced across the forty feet of sky at Peter's chocolate-brown SE5 with its leader streamers fluttering back in the blast from the propeller. Peter never seemed to feel the cold. Even when they had been at school together he had seldom worn an overcoat or scarf. His helmeted head was stretched back, searching the sky.

Marten pulled up the collar of his leather coat,

because his jaw had begun to ache again. The now-habitual speculation about the cause of the ache got him nowhere. Maybe it was the icy wind on the neatly-healed wound. Maybe he'd tensed up too much. Maybe the ache was really in his mind.

An early observation balloon was bobbing slowly up ahead of them, like a huge tethered whale. He caught a glint of reflected light from the basket suspended beneath it. The observer was watching them through his binoculars.

The soft colours of early morning were sharpening, and shapes becoming more clearly defined. It was a good day. Bunched cumulus clouds were drifting, isolated, on the prevailing westerly breeze. Very high in the upper sky delicate threads of icy cirrus streaked the clear blue. You couldn't get an SE5 to fly that high, though you could push it a bit above seventeen and a half thousand feet if you were really determined.

From up there, where the air was getting thin, you could sometimes see the cliffs of England far off to the north-west, and the sun reflecting off the long grey sweep of the Channel. Up there was an altogether different dimension. You felt separated from the affairs of men, in time as well as distance.

Marten made a quick check of his instruments. The engine temperature was still a bit down. The bloody radiator shutters were probably jammed open again. He peered down, feeling the slipstream freezing his face and tearing at his goggles. The Nieppe Forest was below. Ahead the ground began to rise as they approached Messines where the ridge began, curving round and upwards to Passchendaele in the north.

He'd fought his first battle down there with the infantry back in the spring of 1915. And they'd clung to the belief that the war could be over in a few more months. Mary had written that she expected him and Peter and Stephen home for her birthday. That was over two years ago; he'd been in a waterlogged trench on her nineteenth birthday, and a base hospital on her twentieth. Now he was here, decently above it all.

They must be nearly over the front. Peter fired a short burst to test his machine guns and signalled that the others should do the same. In this weather the gun mechanisms sometimes froze. Marten dipped the nose of the machine and pressed the trigger on the control column. The guns thumped briefly, shaking the aeroplane with their recoil.

The earth below was pockmarked with small holes. This sector, to the east of Ypres, changed slightly from day to day as both sides contended for control of the ridge. Off to the right, beyond Armentières, he could see the trench systems winding southwards like a great brown snake towards La Fère, where the front curved south-east, all the way to the Swiss frontier.

Clumps of smoke arose where a Hun battery had thrown over some shells, and he could see answering flashes of British guns hurling shells back. Tracer bullets arced up leisurely from holes below, and he huddled down into the empty security of the canvas-enclosed cockpit. God only knew why Peter always chose to take them over the front at this point. The Hun gunners had spotted them and Smith's SE, flying starboard and slightly behind Peter's, lurched as a shell burst just below it leaving a puff of black smoke. Three more puffs appeared ahead. Marten groaned to himself. The gunners on this section seldom wasted more than a salvo or two, but that was enough to mark their position in the sky and draw in Steiner's vultures.

He glanced across at Peter again, willing him to evade, and Peter changed course very slightly and dropped a couple of hundred feet to throw the gunners' aim. It should have been reassuring, but somehow it unnerved him the way Peter always looked so calm, even at a distance of forty feet and with his face half-covered with his goggles. No doubt about it, it was sometimes difficult not to hate heroes. Particularly if you were a coward.

The jaw had stiffened up now and was aching like a bad tooth. It must be the cold. He beat his gloved hand against his thigh because his fingers were going dead, and glanced anxiously around the sky. Donovan, in the rear, had dropped below them and was giving the dud-engine signal. Peter waved to him and a moment later Donovan banked sharply, falling away, and turned back for home.

Above them and to their left an old RE8 was beating its way back towards the front. Things could be a lot worse. He moved his toes inside his boots to see if he could still feel them. At least he wasn't flying a Harry Tate. A man dedicated to staying alive stood a better chance in an SE5.

The northern extremity of the patrol area lay ahead, clearly defined by the dark, smoking, fetid hump of the Passchendaele Ridge jutting out of the plain. It was like looking down into the bowels of hell. Worse, Steiner's ace flyers were active up there in the early morning, with the sun behind them so you couldn't see them until they were on top of you.

Peter was rocking his wings. His outstretched gloved hand indicated above and to the left. Peter nearly always saw them first. Small black dots, almost invisible against the clouds, took shape. Scout machines a thousand feet above, flying obliquely eastwards, away from them. Marten could feel his mouth going dry. Time to earn his pay.

Peter was climbing and they followed. Marten opened the throttle until he could feel the vibration through his hands. Now they were only three hundred yards behind and below the enemy machines. Pfalz scouts, thank God. Steiner's bunch flew Albatrosses. Maybe these were decoys? There was no time now to search the sky carefully again.

The Germans saw them too late. They broke formation, scattering outwards like startled fish in a pool, and Peter's guns were already raking the slim underbelly of the nearest machine. It swung uncertainly from side to side, then continued straight for several seconds as though caught in the tracer trails. Abruptly it fell sideways, silvery blue vapour jetting from the ruptured fuel tank. The vapour trail turned a dirty brown then flames whooshed back as far as the tail. The small bundled shape of the pilot kicked himself clear and dropped, arms and legs outstretched, getting smaller and smaller.

Now Marten was among the skirmishing machines. Tracers from a pursuing scout flashed across his main plane and he kicked the rudder hard, skidding sideways, then flicked the SE over and dived. He built up speed before dragging back for the zoom upwards. The scout slid past him, one wing down, and as he hauled his machine up he could feel it mushing into a stall. Another Pfalz was above him. He could hold the stall for a couple of seconds, just long enough to blast into the slim belly. Then he glimpsed the yellow tail fin and changed his mind, dropping backwards in a tail slide until the nose fell again.

He looked around quickly to see if Peter was safe, and saw him climbing up from below. The skirmish was over. The Huns were running to the east. Smith, aggressive to the last, chased them then turned back.

Another encounter over and he hadn't contributed anything. Not a blessed thing. He could have got in a good burst at the underside of that Pfalz, but it might have been Yellow Tail himself, and he didn't want to kill him.

12

He fell into place on Peter's left once more.

Strange the way his mouth always dried up like that. And his hands were sweating inside his gloves, even though they were numb with the cold. No doubt there was a reason why they should, somewhere in the mechanism of survival, and surviving was the one thing he was good at.

It was still early and they continued the patrol, south down as far as La Bassée, then north again as far as Poelkapelle. Eventually Peter signalled and they turned for home, across the awful wasteland of the July battles. He wiped his goggles and pulled them back on. God, his jaw ached. Working it from side to side did no good, whisky was the only thing that would fix it. He could see the smudged-brown village and the small church tower of St Eduarde, and the airfield was just ahead.

Peter circled and throttled back. Since Pike and Soames had collided over the hangars, Major Hook had ordered that they land singly, which was a bloody waste of time. Marten waited his turn, blipped the engine a couple of times and bumped down gently on the still dew-damp grass. He slowed then swung the SE around, taxiing back towards the hangars and the waiting Duncan.

Lloyd, still drowsy from bed, sauntered over and joined them as they went into the mess for a second breakfast.

'How did the patrol go, Corby?'

Marten looked at Lloyd who leaned back in his chair, stroking his prematurely bald head. 'Not bad.'

'Don't ask Corby,' Smith intervened. 'He hardly fired his guns.'

'I can't get aggressive this early in the morning,' Marten said. But wasn't it just like bloody Smith to know that he'd landed with his guns still almost fully loaded. You only found out a thing like that if you made it your

13

business. Killer Smith had a hard, sharp, peasant intelligence and he never missed anything.

Drinkwater prodded at his breakfast. 'They've overcooked the sausages again.'

'Think about the poor bloody infantry.' Smith speared his egg with relish. 'What do you suppose they're eating this morning?'

'Now that is something you *could* ask Corby,' Lloyd said.

'Yes, that's right.' Drinkwater paused, his fork raised. 'You were with the infantry, Corby. Up through the ranks, and all that sort of thing. Where did you serve?'

'The Somme, Arras. Here and there.' He didn't feel like talking about it.

Drinkwater sighed and pushed back his plate with distaste. 'I take your point about the poor bloody infantry, Killer, but after all our needs are rather different, aren't they? I wasn't cut out for grubbing around in a wet trench. And war or no war, I cannot reconcile myself to this incinerated food. Another meal like this and I'll have that cook's balls.'

'Wouldn't do you any good,' Lloyd said. 'They'd almost certainly be overdone.'

Peter came in and they all shifted quickly, to give him room at the long table. He should wear one of those Roman helmets, Marten thought, he had the right kind of square-jawed handsome head.

Seating himself, Peter ate with enthusiasm. 'These early patrols always give me a tremendous appetite. Not much happening over the ridge this morning.'

'But you got another one.'

Peter smiled. 'Still keeping everybody's score, Killer?'

'That's your third this month.'

'So it is. I hate to see a fellow jump like that. What do you think, Marten?'

14

'Time for a prayer, between the stirrup and the ground?'

'Isn't that what the crusaders used to say?'

'Let's hope the poor sod had a good breakfast.'

Peter narrowed his eyes. 'I'm never entirely sure when you're joking.'

'Oh, you can count on Corby's irreverence.' Drinkwater signalled for more coffee. 'He has no sense of decorum. If he'd gone to a decent school he might have learned what is good form and what is not.'

It was no good rising to Drinkwater's snobbery, so Marten said, 'We used to have decorum every Monday, between morning prayers and nit inspection.'

'Disgusting!'

Now Drink looked irritated, which was quite satisfying. 'And we used to bawl hymns and kick each other with our hob-nailed boots.'

Peter smiled and winked at him. 'You know perfectly well, Marten, that ours was a very good grammar school.' He glanced around. 'Marten was a much better scholar than I.'

That wasn't true. Peter always excelled at everything, though he often asked your advice, just to make you feel good. That was what defeated you in the end, his artless good nature and his inability to believe you could ever let him down.

'It was a bit off-putting,' Peter went on. 'The way Marten could do very fast calculations in his head. I think that's why he's such a good navigator.'

'Yes, he is that,' Killer Smith conceded reluctantly. 'Corby could find his way back through a sky full of soup. Mind you, I suspect it's more that infernal luck of his. If only somebody would teach him what his guns are for.'

'Their noise offends me.' Marten chose to treat it as a joke.

But Smith wasn't having that. 'You swan around, making up your own rules. It's some kind of bloody game with you, isn't it?'

There was a lull in the conversation all along the table as he stared back at Smith. 'Yes, Killer, it's all a game.'

'Leave it,' Peter interrupted, glancing at them both. And the moment passed.

Benge crept over and seated himself very carefully, trying to keep his head still as if it were a fragile thing precariously balanced on his neck. His eyes were puffy. He looked at his breakfast and groaned.

'God Almighty!'

'Why, Bengy, my old son,' Lloyd exclaimed. And he stroked his bald head again as though trying to encourage the few wispy hairs. 'Feeling a little off colour, are we?'

Benge sipped at his coffee. 'Lloyd, Corby, what did I drink last night?'

'I saw you in The Lantern,' Marten said. 'You were drinking brandy. That was before you went upstairs with the thin, dark girl.'

'God! And I don't even remember!'

'That's probably just as well.' Lloyd grinned across in Marten's direction. 'Corby, can't we find a nice wholesome girl for Benge?'

'I don't know any nice wholesome girls,' he said. 'And if I did I wouldn't let Benge vent his appalling lust on them.'

The pain in his jaw made conversation increasingly difficult, so he left the others and went over to the hangars to see if Duncan had fixed the radiator shutters on the SE. Then he walked back through the thin belt of trees. The sun was drying off the dew and there was a suggestion of winter in the air. He could feel it. Solitary leaves were drifting down, and the trees seemed lethargic, as though settling down for a long sleep. People ought to be allowed

16

to do that, just sleep until the spring came. It was quiet there, but if you stood still and listened you could hear the far-off incessant thump of the guns to the north. The battle had dragged on since July. And for what? Only half the ridge captured, and the bad weather coming.

He walked out from between the trees and along the line of huts to the one he shared with Lloyd and Thompson. Lloyd's elegant, expensive gear was scattered on all three camp beds. It was a bit bloody much having to live with somebody as messy as Lloyd. He scooped up the uniforms and folded them carefully on the bed in the corner.

A three-day-old newspaper, sent out from England, was crumpled on the floor. He picked it up and read the headline, GREAT BRITISH VICTORY AT PASSCHENDAELE RIDGE. That was a bloody lie for a start. He screwed it into a tight ball and threw it in the waste basket. Then he stretched out on his own bed and stared up at the ceiling, trying to make up his mind not to have a drink. But he gave up thinking about it after a minute and eased the flask out of the drawer of his locker.

It was good stuff. The amber liquid slid down his throat, warming him. He opened his lips slightly and hissed inwards. Yes, it was good stuff and already the pain was dulling. He worked his jaw from side to side. The trouble was, one drink never seemed quite enough. And it was funny, because he had been such a prude about drink when he was young, before the war, looking the other way in disgust when Ernie Coppard, the coal heaver from two doors down the mews reeled, massive and red-faced, out of the Masons' Arms on pay nights. God forgive him, yes, he'd been disgusted.

Now, four years later, he was unable to get through the day without whisky, and Ernie Coppard was dead at Ypres. He'd never have thought he could develop a need for whisky in such a short time. He hadn't drunk the stuff until he'd joined the squadron back in June. That was the trouble with being made an officer and a gentleman. It gave you expensive tastes. He closed his eyes. The pain was definitely easing. He could have a little doze until lunchtime.

Oh no, he couldn't. Thompson had clumped in.

'Sorry, were you asleep?'

'No. Just having a rest.'

Thompson was wiping his hands on a rag. He had only arrived in France a fortnight before, and was still all get-up-and-go.

'Do you know, I said to that sergeant, what's 'is name, Baines I think, that my machine isn't rigged properly. It's tail heavy and I have to compensate all the time. And the bloody man said, "Maybe it's the driver." Now what do you make of that?'

Marten grinned to himself and stared up at the ceiling.

Thompson rummaged in his case. 'I won't disturb you. I'm just going to write a letter.'

'Give her my love.'

Thompson smiled shyly. 'As a matter of fact I've been telling her about you and Lloyd. How long have you been flying, Corby?'

'Years. No, I'm lying. It just seems like years. I arrived here at the end of June.'

'But you're ever such a good pilot. Even Killer Smith says so. And you've got a decoration.'

'Got it in the trenches.'

'Did you really! I say, it must be awful to be in the infantry.'

'Awful.' But he smiled as he said it. Then he closed his eyes again because he didn't want to continue the conversation, and he kept his eyes closed until he heard Thompson's pen scratching.

Letters to Thompson, addressed in a round feminine hand, arrived daily, much to the amusement of Lloyd. And that must be the fifth letter Thompson had written to the girl that week. What on earth did he think of to say to her? He envied Thompson in a way. His own links with home seemed tenuous after two and a half years in the war, and he felt an increasing estrangement from the young replacements just out from England, so much so that nowadays he even avoided learning their names. It didn't do to learn a man's name. Once you knew that, you were half-way to feeling responsible for him, and responsibility he could do without.

Thompson's pen was still scratching.

He worked his jaw again. The pain had gone, leaving only a dull numbness. Had he ever been as young as Thompson? In that February, just before the war, he and Peter and Mary and Stephen had all been young then, meeting on Friday nights at the play rehearsals.

He finished work late on Fridays. Mr Laden paid him his wages on the dot of six-forty-five, and returned to his dark inner office where the deep mysteries and movements of the massive coal purchases were arranged. Marten's minimal interest in the coal business faded to nothing as he closed his ledgers and turned down the flaring gas light. Would Mary be at the drama rehearsal? And was it worse to see her than not to see her?

On Friday nights he took a short cut across the huge grimy triangular area of the coal wharves, standing aside for the heavy horse-drawn coal carts. The great tired beasts snorted and steamed at the end of the day as they clattered past the railway sidings and man-made coal mountains. And the mist came at night, drifting over the Grand Union Canal and the coal barges moored up at Laden's Wharf.

He could get out of the wharves at the west exit, near

19

Westbourne Park, and walk through the gas-lit streets to Portobello Road, dirty and crowded with Friday-paid shoppers. Then, panic mounting, turn off past Ladbroke Grove until he reached the arched doorway of the grimy Victorian grammar school, familiar yet alien to him. In all those years as an over-anxious scholarship boy, growing out of his clothes, he had never quite got over the feeling of intrusion as he passed under that arched doorway.

The school smelled of chalk and damp clothes. The narrow corridors were cluttered with dull display cases and dusty exhibits. He had to take a deep breath to calm himself before he entered the hall, where *Mrs Ford's Dilemma* was in rehearsal.

Most of the members of the school drama club were old boys, with a smattering of staff and their wives and daughters. Hutson, the English master, produced and stage-managed. 'Hello, Corby,' he said, and nodded absently.

He glanced around as casually as he could. That was always the worst moment, looking to see if Mary was there. It constantly amazed him that each time he saw her golden hair and her slim boyish figure he experienced the same shocked enchantment. That she was all too aware of the effect she had on him merely added to his scowling embarrassment.

There were three people on the stage, reading their lines from scripts. But Mary Slater, daughter of the headmaster, was standing with Peter and Stephen just to the side of the stage. She was laughing softly at something Stephen was saying, her hand pressed to her mouth. Marten felt a stab of jealousy because bloody Stephen, tall, elegant and superior, was good at making her laugh. Peter was watching the actors, a slight frown on his face.

They were well into Scene Three, so Peter would be fully occupied soon. And Stephen as well. That would give him an opportunity. He groped in his pocket for his script. He could get Mary on her own while Peter and Stephen were on stage together.

It was almost funny, looking back, the way he and Stephen had competed for Mary's attention, while Peter would just saunter over and accept her admiration without thought. In all honesty, he and Stephen hadn't stood much chance because Peter held all the aces.

Peter didn't need other people as much as they needed him, and God knows, that was a direct challenge to any red-blooded girl. Peter didn't have Stephen's carefully cultivated charm, but being entirely sure of himself he didn't seem to need it.

Stephen had the modestly secure future that a small, successful family business promised, but Peter had a strong sense of purpose and he was good at everything. No wonder he'd been made Head of School. Inevitable that he should be awarded a scholarship to university; he was, after all, the most obvious of the school candidates for the year 1912-1913. Yet there was about him a rugged innocence that suggested vulnerability. How could Mary resist such an attractive combination?

Peter would sit, sometimes quite silent, smiling but faintly puzzled at the superficiality of Stephen's sharp, witty observations. Mary would laugh, and glance at all three of them. But her eyes always rested longer on Peter's face.

Marten couldn't remember how he came to be Peter's friend. He'd just noticed one day that Peter was singling him out for conversation. He couldn't imagine why the great Peter West would bother with a gloomy introvert like himself. To be honest, they didn't have much in common, and Peter didn't need to go looking for friends. But there it was.

He had been enormously flattered by Peter's

friendship. But at the same time he'd felt vaguely uneasy, because he had a strong feeling that one day the vulnerable part of Peter's nature would be exposed, and he would have to protect him. Against what? At that time he couldn't have imagined how it would all turn out.

And when had Stephen started to tag along with them? It must have been around the time Mary had entered their lives, by way of a tea party held for members of the sixth form. She had offered them cucumber sandwiches and the prospect of high romance. At the end of the rainy Saturday afternoon she had sat with them, encompassing them with her warmth. Stephen had been at the party too, and a short time after that he'd become the fourth, necessary member of what had seemed then to be a very special group.

What had made them feel special? Probably it had been Mary, though Marten couldn't be sure of that. Maybe it had been all of them together, though there had always been a tension among them because Stephen couldn't bring himself to accept Peter's casual pre-eminence. But they had each known that they were privileged in some way to have each other.

Mary turned and looked towards the entrance of the hall, as though some extra sense had prompted her that he'd arrived. It was funny the way she always did that. And she always knew when he was looking at her, even in a crowded room she would suddenly turn and catch his eye.

She beckoned to him, and Peter turned as he approached. 'Hello, Marten. Good to see you.'

He pretended to interest himself in the performance on the stage. Mary squeezed his arm. 'We were afraid the demands of Mr Laden's coal empire would keep you from our little play.' It was part of her disingenuous charm to imply that what he was doing was far more important.

He grunted. 'Coal cannot keep me from my hour of posturing.'

She turned her head sideways and pouted. 'And I had hoped that you really came to see me.'

Wasn't that just like her?

'Don't frown so,' she said.

Stephen cut in. 'The plot of this play is so ridiculous, how can he help but frown? Even Ellen Terry couldn't make Mrs Ford's dilemma believable.'

Peter shrugged. 'We keep putting on these thin little productions. I told Mr Hutson we should think about trying something with more bite to it.'

'How about Hamlet, with Marten in the title role?' Stephen asked. 'He has a gloomy, soul-searching look.' He smiled and examined his fingernails. 'Or Macbeth perhaps. Peter would make a good Macbeth. *"Vaulting ambition, which o'er leaps itself."'*

Stephen was warming up to being nasty. So Martin said, 'How about Julius Caesar, with you as Cassius?'

Peter had barely heard the exchange. 'We really should alter this scene. Dingle should come in from the left, and Connie should turn and face him. I must have a word with Mr Hutson about it.' And he strode over to the producer.

Stephen yawned, genuinely bored. 'Peter does take it all so seriously.'

'He's usually right.'

'Peter takes everything seriously.' Mary smiled slowly and affectionately at Peter's broad back.

'Oh, quite.' Stephen always got edgy when he was unable to control the drift of the conversation. 'Salt of the earth, our Peter.' He glanced at Mary to see if she was still watching him.

That was the way it was. Whenever Peter left them they ended up talking about him.

It was odd that he should end up here, in France, in Peter's flight.

Marten stirred on his bed. Even the numbness in his jaw had gone now. In a way he wished he'd ended up somewhere else. That feeling persisted: one day Peter's vulnerability would show. It was good to be with him, but out here a close friend was a small, nagging burden. The thought seemed like treachery.

He opened his eyes and looked at his watch. It was midday. Thompson had gone to lunch. Lloyd would be back soon from the mid-morning patrol. He got up and went over to the mess.

Two

IT WAS OFFENSIVE to see Lloyd's boots mixed up with a pile of underwear. Marten began tidying the hut because he couldn't stand living in a pigsty, and jaw-ache made him particularly sensitive to his surroundings.

Lloyd shaved carefully, scowling at the reflection of his prematurely bald head. He turned, razor poised.

'You haven't seen that bottle of cologne of mine, have you? That thieving swine Bates swears he hasn't touched it, but I'll bet he's flogged it, or given it to that black-clad widow of his in the village.'

'God Almighty! Lloyd, the deficiencies in your upbringing are now revealed. You are completely incapable of looking after yourself.' Marten pulled the bottle of cologne from under a pile of Lloyd's shirts, then stacked the shirts on Lloyd's bed. 'Look at this! Shirts, boots, underwear, opened parcel from Fortnum and Mason. How can you live this way? What do you want with all this gear anyway? Nobody needs two pairs of riding boots.'

'What you mean is that *you* don't need two pairs of riding boots.' Lloyd wiped his dirty razor on a towel and swabbed his face. 'It is, as you say, a matter of upbringing, and of course background. As you were dragged up in the gutters of North Paddington the requirements of an English middle-class gentleman are incomprehensible to you. Do be a good chap and pass me one of those shirts. I'll wager Bates hasn't ironed them properly.'

'The poor sod is heading for a nervous breakdown. He's so busy trying to keep this hut tidy and your gear in order he barely has time to clean my boots. And young Thompson doesn't even get a look in. His boots haven't been cleaned for days. What are you getting dressed up for, anyway?'

Lloyd pulled on his shirt and began buttoning it, still scowling at his bald head in the mirror. 'There's a nice plump girl with a stupendous bosom in the estaminet in Béthune.' He cupped his hands over his chest. 'Stupendous! Bengy and I are going to run over there for a spot of lunch. We've scrounged a vehicle from the transport pool. Want to come?'

'No thanks. The last time I went drinking in Béthune with you two, Benge threw up in the town square. I was very embarrassed. And on the way back we had to stop the Crossley five times so that Benge could get out and pee. Anyway I'm low on cash. I've got just enough for a start in a poker game.'

'It wasn't five times, it was only four. Cash is no problem. I'll stand you.'

'Thanks anyway, but I need my poker winnings to subsidise my drinking habit.'

'Yes, you are hitting it rather hard, and you're smoking too much.' Lloyd donned his peaked cap and suddenly looked his true age of twenty-four. He stopped scowling. 'You are all right, aren't you?'

'Fine.'

'Jaw giving you any trouble?'

'I'm all right.'

Lloyd looked at him steadily for a moment. 'You really ought to get it seen to, you know.'

Marten just nodded. Only Lloyd and Peter knew about his jaw. There was no point in talking about it.

'I hear Peter scored again. Let's see, that must be his eleventh kill.' Lloyd adjusted his tie.

'Yes. A Pfalz. It burst into flames at about five

26

thousand feet, and the poor bloody Hun pitched himself over the side.'

'It's a long way to drop. But better that than to burn.' Lloyd curled his lip slightly, staring again into the mirror. 'How do you think I would look with a moustache?'

'Appalling.'

'You'd think they'd give us parachutes, wouldn't you? I mean, it's not a matter of the weight any more. If they can stick four twenty-pound Cooper bombs under the fuselage, they could give us parachutes that weigh less than that.'

He felt sour. 'I suppose they think we'd be less inclined to save the plane if we could safely jump from it.'

'Exactly.' Lloyd patted his tunic pockets. 'Now you're sure you won't come with us? You ought to get out more, you're becoming a hermit. Plenty of room in the car.'

'No. I'm going to tidy this place up, then play poker.'

'Right.' Lloyd paused for a moment, making a last inspection of himself, perhaps thinking how to phrase his parting comment. 'I dare say you'll win at cards. You usually do. But you need some other diversion you know, like a woman, or religion.'

'Get out of here.'

A woman or religion? You could lose yourself in either. And being an incurable bloody romantic he could easily confuse one with the other. He *was* religious, in his own fashion. Up above the alto cumulus the feeling was quite strong that God existed. And it didn't much matter what happened, because there was a purpose to it all, even if he couldn't discern it. The trouble was, he could never quite catch the feeling when he was down on the ground.

Down here, man's special place in the world seemed obvious. Up there it was irrelevant. Mortal, immortal? That didn't much matter either. Man was a seeker. The aeroplane, flying higher and faster than the birds, proved that. But what was wondrous about man was his capacity for being deliberately irrational. Not content with a machine that would soar into the sky, he went and stuck a machine gun on it. A very peculiar animal.

They crowded into Donovan's hut and played around the upturned packing case that Donovan used as a card table.

Marten didn't really enjoy playing poker, but he'd won so consistently in the last few months that it was worth his while. It was uncanny the way the cards favoured him, frightening almost. Could it last? Or were THEY saving something particularly nasty for him by way of come-uppance? The cards had given impetus to the legend of 'Bloody Corby's Luck.'

Drinkwater came in and joined them. He had a studied carelessness in his dress. There were leather patches on the elbows of his perfectly-cut tunic. They drew for seats and Donovan shuffled and dealt. Templer stood behind, watching the game, a slight smile on his handsome face.

Donovan was cursing his dud engine. 'When I made my temporary peace with the English and came over from Ireland to fight their war for them, I thought the least I could expect would be good equipment. When are we going to get the modified SE5? 56 Squadron got theirs in March.'

Lewis fumbled with his cards and whistled tunelessly a few bars of *The Dying Aviator*. He had a theory that whistling broke Bloody Corby's Luck. 'They've had a lot of trouble with the engines. Faulty reduction gears. Did you hear about 56 Squadron shooting down Werner Voss yesterday?'

Drinkwater looked pained. 'Lewis, is this another one of your stories?'

'Of course it is.' Killer Smith glared down at his cards. 'Lying sod.'

'It's true.' Lewis looked around. 'Honest! Voss took on the whole squadron, then Rhys-Davids finally plugged him. Roper told me so this morning.'

The hand was over and the deal passed to Drinkwater, who glanced at Lewis as he began shuffling the cards. 'Last week you put the story round that Roper got his job as Recording Officer for this squadron because he's obscurely related to General Trenchard, and poor old Roper couldn't understand why all and sundry were actually listening to him for a change. Donovan even bought him a drink. Then Canning sneaked a look at Roper's service record and discovered that the poor sod doesn't fly any more because he's got piles. And *that* is why he was made the Recording Officer for this squadron.'

Lewis whistled a few more bars, frowning at his cards. 'Ah, but I was the first to tell you that Roper's piles are resisting the most bizarre medical treatment. Honestly, you wouldn't believe . . . '

'You're bloody right we wouldn't,' Smith growled. 'And I'll believe that Voss is dead when I see it in print.'

'Il n'y a pas de morts.' Donovan frowned at his cards. 'It's Steiner that I worry about.'

Smith was getting impatient. 'Get on with the game, for God's sake.'

It was funny how the mention of Steiner's name made his gut tighten up. A conditioned reflex, like Pavlov and his dogs. The thought of those pale blue Albatrosses, beautiful like sharks, with their spade-shaped tails and raked-back underfins triggering a surge of pain in his jaw. It was probably all in his mind, the pain, imagined because it offered a way out of flying the next patrol, if he cared to take it.

Donovan sighed and dropped out. 'This game is too hot for a simple Irish lad.'

Drinkwater changed his position slightly, leaning forward casually and glancing at the faces of the other players. That meant he'd got a good hand. Lewis stopped whistling and started to look nervous, which meant he'd got a fairly good hand too, but wasn't sure.

It would be easy to find out what Lewis had got. Marten doubled.

Smith snarled and threw his cards face down. 'I'm out.'

Lewis dithered a moment and threw his in as well.

That was pretty much what he'd expected. It left just him and Drinkwater to contest the pot. Bloody uncanny, wasn't it? Sometimes it was as if he knew the end of the round even before the deal. So he said, 'I'll play these.'

Drinkwater nodded. 'Playing these.'

It was getting a bit tense now, and he'd have to finish it quickly because it was almost time to go on patrol. He doubled.

Drinkwater paused, unable to make up his mind whether to throw good money after bad. 'I'll see you.' He pushed more coins into the pot.

When you knew you were going to win it all became quite mechanical. He spread out his Full House. Drinkwater shrugged in disgust and threw down a flush.

Which was worse, winning or losing? One day, when he least expected it, there would come the moment of reckoning. He scooped the winnings into his hat.

'You jammy sod.' Lewis had a look of shocked surprise.

Smith, exasperated, snapped up the cards and slid them back in the box. 'How the hell does he do it?'

'Corby made a pact with the devil, George,' Drinkwater said. 'Come on, we've only got about ten minutes to take-off.'

Drinkwater was the only man in the squadron who called Smith by his first name. The two of them left together, walking over to the hut they shared with Canning. Marten followed them, on his way to his own hut. It was very odd, he thought. Normally Drinkwater avoided close association with those whom he considered socially inadequate, and socially Smith was a disaster. Before the war he had been an engineering apprentice at Petter's in Yeovil. When old Petter founded Westland Aircraft, Smith moved over into seaplane-building. He'd been a skilled fitter for a year then. Somehow he'd learned how to fly. So they commissioned him into the Flying Corps.

You wouldn't find a more unlikely pair than Smith and Drinkwater, but they had a curious regard for each other. People were full of contradictions. There was nothing logical about his own behaviour, was there? Why would a coward stay out here? He could play up his damaged jaw and get sent home. But he wouldn't. Bloody mad, wasn't he?

Thompson watched him as he threw his poker winnings down on the bed and began pulling on his sheepskin boots.

'How much did you win this time?'

'I don't know. I haven't counted it.'

Thompson shook his head, frowning down at the pile of notes and coins. 'I hope you don't mind me saying this, Corby, but you are an odd fellow. Why don't you ever count your winnings?'

'If you want to know how much I've won, you count it. But don't tell me.' He left the money on the bed and walked quickly towards the hangars. Not counting the winnings was one of his numerous superstitions. As if it could possibly make any difference. But he wasn't going to test his luck. God knows, there were hazards enough.

Peter was standing by his machine and frowning up at the sky. Most men looked clumsy, weighed down by bulky flying clothes, but Peter looked completely at ease.

'Hello, Marten. How fast do you think those clouds are moving?' He turned attentively, waiting for a reply. It was a way he had, of making you feel important. He would listen carefully to what you said, and nod seriously, even if you were just giving him your opinion on the quality of the beer you were drinking, or what you would do if you were General Trenchard. But then Peter knew that other people were less self-sufficient than he, and needed to be listened to. It was this appreciation of the requirements of lesser mortals that made him so endearing. He ascribed to each individual a particular and unique dignity.

Now, with his helmeted head turned up to the sky, Peter had the appearance of a young medieval prince, ready to lead the host to glory.

There wasn't much glory in it. Peter led them over the front at eleven thousand feet. You could see the curvature of the Earth from that height, and the whole of the patrol area from Ypres down to La Bassée, and beyond that the black country of mines, slag heaps and blast furnaces. The ground below appeared flat, but if you looked carefully you could pick out the rolling chalk hills among the dikes and sluggish rivers of the broad, waterlogged plain. The trenches snaked between the high wooded hump of Mount Kemmel and the long, curved ridge leading up to Passchendaele.

Then Martin noticed the oil pressure gauge.

The needle had dropped back from its normal position. He had lost a lot of pressure. The reading on the temperature gauge was still normal. The sudden knot in his stomach eased a little. The engine was still running smoothly. Perhaps the gauge was faulty. He tapped the glass with his gloved hand. No. The needle had dropped further.

He daren't risk staying with the others. He fired a quick burst with his guns to attract Peter's attention, then gave the dud-engine signal. Peter nodded vigorously and waved across the forty feet of sky.

He made a slow turn, trying not to lose too much height, and fighting down the impulse to hurry his movements. He would have to reduce his speed to ease the strain on the engine, but hold his altitude for the long glide back if the engine seized up.

The sun was in front of him now, moving down into the west, and he felt alone and very vulnerable, glancing around anxiously in the bright afternoon sunlight. He was a good eight miles over, and there was a steady wind blowing in from the west. If the engine stopped now, maybe he hadn't enough height to get back over to the British side.

The needle had dropped back a little more, but the engine was still running smoothly. Maybe there was no oil leak. It could be a faulty pressure pump. Either way, the engine could stop at any moment. And if he'd got a leak, the oil could be seeping along the underside of the fuselage. Sparks from the exhaust could ignite it and the plane would burn like a torch.

It was no good telling himself, for the thousandth time, that he was a fool, even though it was true. He could have stayed in England after his jaw had mended. Other jaw cases, no worse than his, had been in hospital eight months or more, and then got their discharge. He deserved all he got. But please God, don't let the plane catch fire.

Ypres lay ahead, and he could see the sun glinting on the Zillebeke lake just to the south of the town. He began to breathe a little easier. At least he could glide that far, providing no Huns were stalking him. He couldn't evade them if they were up there now, watching him.

The engine was beginning to run hot and he thought he could detect a change, a roughness in its sound. He throttled back and kept the nose just above stalling angle. Then the controls began to feel soggy so he lost altitude to pick up speed. Black puffs of smoke appeared just ahead of him as the ground gunners hurled up a salvo of shells. He could smell the acrid, spent explosive as he crossed the front. Then he was over his own side.

He was low over the British support trenches, and the engine missed, then fired again, briefly gouting out smoke from its exhausts. It was like that first patrol he'd flown, when he'd lost sight of Peter, and the yellow-tailed Pfalz had chased him, like a ferret chasing a rabbit, fifty feet over the startled infantrymen peering up at them. He'd swung from side to side because he'd been so green he hadn't known what else to do. And Yellow Tail, with consummate ease, manoeuvred alongside and waved across at him and grinned before turning back to his own side. Why had he done that? Why hadn't he shot him?

The knot in his stomach had eased appreciably now. Maybe he could get all the way home? The pressure was still dropping, but quite slowly. He would lose more height, but maintain enough altitude for a long glide if it became necessary. That would give him time to look for a field to put down in.

Back in July he'd watched Peter glide all the way back, from Armentières to the airfield. They'd grouped themselves around him, easing back on the throttles to keep pace with him. Peter had seemed quite unconcerned, raising his gloved hand from time to time to indicate that he was all right. It was odd how Peter's small gestures remained vividly in the mind.

The engine was running very hot though the pressure had dropped only a fraction since he'd crossed the front. He kept south of the Nieppe Forest because he didn't fancy ploughing down among the trees. He would make it all the way home now. St Eduarde lay just the other side of the canal. No engine could be so bitchy that it would die on him after he'd nursed it this far, could it?

The square church tower and the sugar beet factory were below him. He wouldn't chance circling the airfield. All right, engine, you can pack up now if you really feel you have to, he thought. And it did. It clattered for a moment then stopped, with the propeller fixed rigidly dead. He fired off a red flare and glided down onto the airfield. Bloody Corby's Luck still held.

With the cowling stripped off, the aeroplane looked strangely unflyable. He stood and watched Duncan's hunched shoulders as the mechanic delved into the chewed-up scrap metal of his engine.

Duncan turned. 'It's finished, Mr Corby. But it's been past its best for some time.'

Marten knew that. He'd done that engine in, running it flat out all the way back from Roulers to Ypres that time. 'Well, I can't get over the front with that,' he said. 'Not unless I climb out and push it.'

Duncan smiled patiently.

'So you'll fit me a new engine?'

Duncan pursed his lips and shook his head. He quite enjoyed being a doom merchant. 'Reconditioned, sir. New one hundred and fifty horse power Hispanos are like gold dust.'

Wouldn't you know it? Marten left Duncan and his other mechanic up to their elbows in oil and scrap metal.

He crossed the cinder apron in front of the Nissen workshops and flapping canvas hangars. Why didn't somebody clean up all the aeroplane junk scattered about?

35

And why did untidiness upset him so? There was the mainplane off an old BE2. God knows where that had come from. And the wrecked engine from Pike's SE5 looked as if it would stay there until it rotted, as, no doubt, poor old Pike was now rotting. He stuck his hands in his pockets and scuffed the cinders as he walked back to the hut.

Nobody was there. Bates had dropped the mail in. There were two letters for Thompson of course, both in the same firm, schoolgirlish hand. And one letter for himself. It was from his mother.

She wrote in short sentences. There were queues for meat and sugar. The German Gotha bombers had been raiding London at night, but he wasn't to worry about her or his father. Miss Stacey sent her good wishes. His father's limp had worsened because of the cold weather. Fred Payne from next door had been killed in action.

God Almighty! Poor old Fred! He felt a stab of guilt. Fred had been a good friend when they were at the elementary school together. Then he'd won the scholarship for admission to the grammar school, leaving Fred behind. It hadn't been quite the same after that. But Fred had stood by him when all the other lads in the mews ganged up on him for being a toffee-nosed grammar school kid. No good to protest that he wasn't toffee-nosed. They all knew, didn't they, that now he was different from them. The Torquay Street gang duffed him every night until he learned to take a different route home.

He and Fred still kicked the football in the mews, and stood together watching the farrier shoeing Mr Laden's great coal horses. But there had been the homework to do. Then, when they were fourteen, Fred had gone to work in the coal yards, and there wasn't much time, and only occasional meetings in the mews, and a quick kick with the ball. These too became rare. After he took up with Peter and Mary and Stephen he hardly saw Fred at all.

He finished reading the letter and glanced back to the single sentence, *Miss Stacey sends her good wishes*. Miss Stacey used to make him feel . . . what was the word? Gauche. She'd taken the flat opposite, above the printers. She intrigued him. Fred would pause from smashing the ball at the dustbin and openly gawp at her. She rarely gave the impression that she had noticed them.

Miss Stacey was studying to be a pharmacist then, and that placed her a cut above the other mews dwellers. Yet for all that, she seemed to fit in. The men fancied her because she was long-legged and curved nicely in all the right places. Also, she presented an interesting challenge, what with her education and her stylish clothes. Why she had chosen to live in the mews was the subject of endless speculation. Several of the local unmarried hopefuls had tried their luck with her, but only young David Solomons, the ship's steward on leave, seemed to get anywhere. And that hadn't lasted long because the following Sunday she'd been seen out with Jobling, the well-to-do widower who owned the chemist shop in Kinkaid Street. David Solomons had gone back to sea the following day, so nobody knew how he felt about it.

What was surprising was the way most of the women, notoriously clannish in the mews, appeared to accept her. Maybe it was because, with her professional status, she represented the emancipation of their down-trodden sex. With the exception of Sid Lovatt, whose wife was large and menacing, the men of the mews kept their women severely in their place.

Maybe it was because it was cheaper to talk to her about their ailments than to go to the doctor. Whatever the case, she listened to them in that curiously intent way of hers. It was strange the way she did that. He'd noticed it because he'd studied Miss Stacey quite carefully. When she smiled at something one of them said, you could see a flash of white teeth, uneven because the eye teeth were longer than the others.

Life was, after all, a bit raw in the mews. So he could think of only one reason why she had come to live among them. She was really stuck-up. She must see herself as some kind of missionary among the savages. Looking back, it was odd. It had never occurred to him that somebody like her might *want* to live there.

Two nights after the Titanic went down, old Mr Solomons stumbled along the mews clutching the newspaper with its lists of known drowned, and sobbed, making huge ugly gulping sounds. And they all knew that David Solomons was dead. The neighbours had stood and watched, concerned but unable to approach him because he was a Jew and different from them.

Jean Stacey had run out from her flat and put her arm round the old man's shoulders. She led him along the cobbles to his rag-picker's shop at the end of the mews. And almost unbelievably, she went up the stairway with him to his lodgings above the shop. Nobody else in the mews had ever gone, or even wanted to go up there. Miss Stacey was a puzzle, allowing her compassion to show that way, while all the mews watched. But then, she was probably being a missionary again.

Mixed feelings of guilt and lust had plagued after the night he'd entered his small darkened bedroom and, through the chink in her curtains across the mews, seen her undressing before the fire. The image was still sharp in his mind after all this time. Frozen, fascinated, he had watched her release her long shiny black hair. It fell over her white shoulders and large breasts. She stroked her hair with a brush, then paused, staring into the fire before rising and turning to flick the curtains together.

It was strange, the sharp feeling of exclusion when the curtains closed. Why should he feel excluded? It didn't make sense, because he was in love with Mary Slater, the headmaster's daughter. But after that he hated the men who took her out. Jobling, wealthy and middle-aged, called from time to time, looking down his nose at the dustbins. And Laden's idle, feckless son sometimes came to collect her in his fast, sporty touring car. But most of the men were not from the neighbourhood. Their clothes and manner set them apart.

The night before Fred Payne went off to join the army, Marten had meant to go and say goodbye to him. But as he paused before Mrs Payne's door he had seen Miss Stacey and his father passing under the flaring gas lamp at the mews end. She was walking slowly, keeping pace with the limping figure at her side. He'd turned away from Mrs Payne's door, uncertain what to do, because he would be trapped now, in conversation with her and his father.

The old man had seen him and called out. He stood there, helpless, while they came towards him.

'Hello lad. I kept Miss Stacey company along past the wharves. Dangerous there on a dark night.' Huge and grimy from his day in the wharves, the old man smelled of sweat and coal dust. He scratched his head through his dirty cloth cap. 'It's rough around here and we have to look after the most handsome young woman in the neighbourhood, don't we? Mind you, if I was twenty years younger, it might be me you'd have had to worry about.' He grinned at her. He had a brash, sure charm that always seemed to work.

Miss Stacey's eyes lighted with amusement. She tilted her head on one side and smiled. 'Ten years perhaps?'

'Well, I don't move as fast as I used, not when the damp gets into my leg.' He sighed and thumped his thigh with his large fist. 'The cold gets into a man. And old

wounds ache and stir the memory. I had eight years with
the army in India, three of them on the North-West
Frontier. Then I got this.' He slapped his leg again with his
hand. 'And they shipped me home.'

Miss Stacey didn't say anything. She stood, listening
expectantly for the old man to finish his story, as if
nothing was more important to her.

'I often think of India now,' he said. 'When the cold
gets into my bones and the rain soaks us in the coal yards.
It was always hot there. When you're young the bad times
and the good seem so entwined that the bad don't matter
so much.'

Miss Stacey watched the old man's face, smiling.
'"Somewhere east of Suez, where the best is like the
worst."'

'Ah, you've read Kipling. But then you're a scholar.'
He grinned at her, then jerked his head. 'My boy here is
the scholar in our family. Got to the grammar school, he
did.'

Oh God, was the old man going to go on about his
getting the scholarship?

'Clever boy,' she said. She knew he was embarrassed,
and she was amused.

'Got to go,' the old man said. 'I'll have the wife after
me if she knows I'm standing here talking to a pretty girl.'

She laughed softly. Marten envied the old man his
ability to make Miss Stacey's eyes go warm like that.

'I think Mrs Corby trusts you,' she said. 'Providing
you're not too far out of her sight. But what of all my
boyfriends? They'll be very respectful when they hear Jack
Corby escorted me home.'

It seemed that she had her interest entirely on the old
man, until the moment of parting. That wasn't surprising,
because the old man had done all the talking, while
Marten hadn't said a word. Then she turned, and her eyes

40

rested on his for just a fraction longer than was necessary. And yes, she was amused. 'Goodnight Marten.' That was all she said.

'Nice young woman, that,' the old man grunted. He narrowed his eyes, smiling to himself, then shrugged. 'Come on, lad.'

'She's stuck up. And she'll go out with anybody who has money.'

The old man just grinned and didn't say anything.

They climbed the steep, narrow stairway to the small flat above the stable. There was no denying it, he was clumsy and awkward. He hadn't managed to think of one intelligent thing to say. And the old man, in his filthy clothes, had managed to charm her the way he charmed everyone.

The smell of coal dust pervaded the tiny, warm, polished parlour. He'd always lived here, and felt safe. But the regimental trophies and the medals, and the large sepia photography of his father, in tightly-buttoned tunic and with sergeant's stripes on his sleeve, aroused in him a curious mix of admiration and unease. He was unsure he could ever match that figure.

He sat at the table as his mother fussed and tutted and put out the supper, listening to the loud voice from the kitchen, where the old man was washing the grime of the yards from his body. The feeling of inadequacy following the encounter with Miss Stacey began to subside. Only then did he remember Fred Payne, packing his cardboard suitcase in readiness for his departure for the army. It was too late to go and see him now. But he'd see him when he came on leave, wouldn't he? Yes, he'd go out with Fred then.

His father and mother were talking but he hardly heard, because he was suddenly very conscious of the strangeness and excitement of human relationships. The outcomes were so unpredictable. Anything could happen. He would see Mary again on Friday and steer her away from Peter and Stephen for a while.

Through the wall he could hear Sid Lovatt singing, trying to annoy his wife. Fred was next door on the other side, getting ready to start his new life as a soldier. Across the mews the cool, sure Miss Stacey would be standing in front of the fire, brushing her long black hair. Or perhaps she would be undressing! He felt his face flush and quickly stifled the thought. The whole spring and summer of 1914 lay ahead, rich with an immense range of possibilities.

Three

MARTEN STARED gloomily out of the hut window at the drizzle. The clear bright autumn days had suddenly gone. Dark clouds scudded low across the sky and the rain had come, cold and biting, drenching the airfield and turning dust-dry roads and farmlands into heavy yellow mud. You had to count your blessings though. They hadn't flown for two days. The weather people said it might clear by the afternoon, and if that happened Major Hook would have them all in the air regardless of the state of the field.

The sudden cold seemed to have crept into his soul. He lit a cigarette. It was his sixth that morning. He couldn't remember feeling so down. It wasn't like being afraid to fly the patrols, then at least there was a tension within him. Now he felt numbly indifferent. It wasn't just the weather. Canning going like that, a burst tyre and the machine turning over, and a dozen mechanics trying to lever the wreck off the crushed body. Then losing at cards, and the icy feeling inside when he saw how much Smith and Lewis and Drinkwater were enjoying watching his luck change. Would they enjoy the same unspoken satisfaction in seeing him shot down?

But the letter from Mary had depressed him most. He had accepted that she and Peter would marry when it was all over. It had looked that way since the winter of 1914, when Peter came home on leave, very smart in his well-cut Special Reserve uniform. And Mary very proud of him, hanging on his arm and going everywhere with him. It had all been so bloody inevitable. So he'd gone and enlisted in the East Surrey Regiment the next day because it seemed the most obvious thing to do. Recently he'd reached the point where, much of the time, he really didn't mind any more. Of course he was still in love with Mary, there was no denying that.

Now it all looked different. There had been a very long gap, then that last letter from her, full of doubts. Stephen had been badly wounded in the fighting for St Julien and her cousin had been killed at Polygon Wood. Her younger brother had enlisted, despite her pleas. She hadn't seen Peter for over six months. His leave was surely due, but she feared that the war might have changed them both.

Marten was startled. No, he'd go further: he was shocked. This wasn't the way he remembered her. She'd always insisted that they would all get through the war and pick up the threads of their lives again. He and Peter had changed in some ways, of course they had, but surely not Mary? He and Peter would go home together when it was all over. Peter would marry Mary, and he would visit them and take presents to their children.

So he broke a rule of long standing, not to get involved in other people's affairs, and went to have a chat with Peter.

Peter was busy, trying to catch up with his paperwork. He had a pen in one hand and was flicking through folders with the other.

'Go on, go on. I'm listening.'

'She's depressed, and I think you ought to get some leave.'

'Depressed, you say?' Peter scribbled something on one of the files. 'Yes, I know she's feeling a little low, but she's much more determined than you give her credit for. She'll pull herself together in a day or two. The war takes it out of all of us.' He paused. 'She really ought to take up some kind of war work. What do you think would suit her?'

'Ah, for God's sake, Peter! You've been out here for months. Your leave is well overdue. Mary needs to see you.'

Peter shook his head. 'No. You've got it out of proportion. My place is here. I can't scuttle home just because Mary's depressed. After all, there are thousands of other girls in the same position.' He began scratching with his pen again. 'I'll suggest to her that she gets a job. Thanks for looking in, Marten.' He glanced up. 'You're a good fellow, concerning yourself about Mary and me. Don't worry. It will be all right. Anything else on your mind? Are you sure? Fine then, I'll see you later.'

For God's sake! A written suggestion to Mary that she should take up war work! To be brutally honest, Mary wasn't the war-work type. He couldn't picture her as a VAD, or slopping up tea in a canteen for soldiers. Mary was surely apart from all that. She'd been something constant and shining in his life.

But all of a sudden he couldn't think of her in the old way any more. Mary was an attractive young woman, and she was fit. Perhaps Peter was right, and she should be doing something useful.

It was inevitable that sooner or later he would have to put aside his bloody infantile notions of Mary, but at the same time he felt robbed of something important. That image of her had kept him going through some bad times. And he was a bit resentful, admittedly without just cause, that Peter's common-sense reaction should have undermined that image.

Peter was right. He'd got it out of proportion. How bloody childish he was. But he'd always been like that, romanticising people, then being vaguely disappointed when they turned out to be human after all. Like that time at the Sixth Form party and dance. Peter had disappeared, with Mary of course, and he'd gone to find him because the headmaster wanted Peter to squire round one of the lady governors. He'd found them in the darkened cloakroom, Peter kissing Mary passionately, and she moaning softly. He'd crept away without them seeing him. He'd felt a bit shocked, because he hadn't thought of their relationship in physical terms. Absurd. That's what he was.

The drizzle had ceased. He continued to stare out of the window until Lloyd and Thompson came into the hut.

'Yes, my old son.' Lloyd clapped him on the shoulder. 'The rain has stopped and the jig is up. The field is soaking and you may be up to your backside in mud. But we fly this afternoon, and the first man who says Major Hook is a bastard gets fifty-six days in the glasshouse.'

Lloyd went over to the mirror and began examining the stubble of his new moustache. 'What do you think of it?' He began brushing the whiskers outwards with no noticeable effect.

Marten went over to Lloyd and peered closely at the moustache. 'I'm not sure yet. Thompson, you'd better get a doctor. It might be serious.'

Lloyd snorted with disgust and peered into the mirror again. Marten went back to the window and stared gloomily out. Only a bloody maniac would try to get the squadron off the field immediately after all that rain. It was like a quagmire out there.

Thompson joined him. 'Killer Smith says we'll have to take off north to south, regardless of the direction of the wind, so as to avoid that badly drained patch.'

He could throw in a bit of gratuitous advice because it didn't cost anything. 'Yes. And try to get your wheels up before you reach that bit where it begins to slope down.'

'You mean that bit where Canning was kill . . . '

'That's right.' He cut in quickly because he didn't want to hear Thompson say it. He could feel Thompson glancing at him, concerned, so he changed the subject.

'How's your girl, Thompson?'

'Oh, she's fine.' Thompson's face softened. 'She's fine.'

'You're a bit secretive about her,' Lloyd said. 'What's she like?'

Thompson hesitated. 'I don't know how to describe her without resorting to clichés.'

'Well, show us a picture of her,' Lloyd said.

Thompson paused for a moment. 'All right. She had this one taken for me just before I left for France.' He opened his wallet and took out a sepia photograph.

'Thompson, my old son, how on earth did you manage it!'

Lloyd and Marten stared at the girl's calm face. The eyes were soft but the mouth was firm. With her hair hanging loosely over her shoulders. She looked surprisingly like Mary.

Marten patted Thompson on the back. 'You're a very lucky fellow, but I'm sure you deserve her.' It was as if he were outside himself, watching the three of them looking at the photograph.

Lloyd was frowning slightly. 'She looks very young.'

'Yes. She's still at school, in the sixth form.'

'Well, you're a dark horse, I must say. If you want any advice, just ask your old Uncle Lloyd. Don't ask Corby, he's such a doom-ridden sod. He's been in the war too long, you see.'

Thompson grinned. 'I don't know why you fellows keep treating me like an innocent nephew. You're only twenty-four, Lloyd. And Corby isn't yet twenty-one.'

Lloyd assumed a look of horror. 'Did you hear that, Corby? The lad's suggesting that he isn't innocent after all. I don't know what he's been up to with that poor girl, but I'll bet it's illegal.'

He went back to the mirror and began rubbing hair restorer into his shiny scalp. 'I would hate to be committed to one girl. It would be such a waste of me.' He paused, squeezing a spot on his chin. 'That girl in the estaminet in Béthune.' He cupped his hands on his chest. 'I think she's beginning to show some interest.'

'Somebody should warn her.' Marten went to the window again. Yes, the visibility was clearing. They would fly that afternoon.

Lloyd smoothed his scalp, scowling blackly at his reflection. 'Nothing can save her from the lone flyer, scourge of the virgins of Cheltenham Spa.'

'To what do you attribute your horrifying success?'

'Oh, good breeding, a natural charm, clean living, and my daddy's money.'

'You're lucky. I have to win my money at poker. Come on, let's take a walk and leave Thompson to his letter-writing.'

They walked round by the rough, muddy cart track towards St Eduarde. The wind was blustery. Marten pulled up his greatcoat collar. Lloyd was silent, as if trying to decide how to frame his thoughts.

'Donovan tells me you lost heavily at poker?'

'Not too heavily. I'm still well ahead.'

'Consistently winning doesn't make you very popular.'

'I suspect I wouldn't be very popular even if I didn't win.'

'Well, let's be honest.' Lloyd sunk his hands deep into his pockets. 'You are a bloody loner, and nothing worries people more than a loner who makes up his own set of rules. Killer Smith may be a tactless, blunt baboon, but he doesn't miss much. I heard him telling Drinkwater and Templer that you got between him and a Pfalz the other day, but you didn't shoot at it.'

Lloyd looked puzzled. 'You can see their point of view, can't you? You seem to monopolise what luck there is. And you're the best pilot among us – the Killer would dearly love to be able to do what you do with an aeroplane. Yet you haven't shot any Huns down. Much worse, as far as they're concerned, you don't seem to care very much.'

Not quite the case; these days the question was never far from his thoughts. 'In the trenches I watched a lot of men die.' The extent to which a human body can be mangled by shell splinters, bullets or bayonet thrusts, and still remain conscious had to be witnessed to be believed. 'The blood and death stay with you.'

'I can imagine.'

'No, Lloyd, you can't begin to imagine it. Because up there, among the clouds, we're nicely distanced from those we kill or mutilate.'

'Whether we actually see the other fellow die is neither here nor there. We were trained to shoot down Huns. It's not for us to think about it, we just do our job as efficiently as we can.'

'And become machines – killing machines.'

'Unhappily that is our function. Temporarily we are killing machines. But frankly, Corby, I don't know why you stay out here. That jaw of yours is giving you a lot of trouble.'

'Oh, didn't I tell you? It's my sense of high purpose.' He grinned as he said it, turning it into a joke. Though it wasn't a joke. There were a number of jumbled reasons that added up to a compulsion to stay in France, though they made no real sense. Perhaps staying, like trying to capture and hold the Passchendaele Ridge, was a purpose in itself. 'We're here because we're here because we're here because we're here.'

'I'll write that on your tombstone,' Lloyd said.

They reached St Eduarde. The blustery wind was drying the sad, stained houses. There were no young men to be seen. Verdun had swallowed them all up. A girl dressed in black, leading a small child, looked at him with frank invitation. Her eyes were warm with promise and her breasts large beneath her shapeless dress. Marten smiled at her, and at the child who stared back stonily.

'God, what a war!' he said. 'She's still in her winter widow's weeds and she's already planning her spring campaign.'

'She knows how to survive.'

He suddenly wanted Miss Stacey.

Wanting Miss Stacey always sharpened those images of his youth in the mews. The sensuous body contrasting with her cool, direct gaze confused him. Fred Payne used to make jokes about her, just to make him blush. Did she know? Yes, she must have bloody well known. Fred had waved to her when she was leaning across her window sill, arm outstretched, watering the flowers in the window box. She smiled when Fred turned and deliberately banged his head against the wall, as if the sight of her was driving him potty with desire. Her arm remained outstretched, pulling tight the dress across the roundness of her. Was she intentionally prolonging that posture, or was she just mildly amused and thinking about her daffodils? Whatever her intention, he'd had another sleepless night, trying hard to submerge that image by thinking about Mary's fair hair and slim, boyish figure.

But it wasn't just that he lusted after Miss Stacey. He frowned down at the ground as he walked. He wanted to talk to her. He'd wanted to talk to her that time he'd met her in the park, when he was just an infantryman, home on leave from France after the Somme battles. He'd gone to the park because he felt out of place in the streets crowded with civilians. They were all so friendly to soldiers, doing their bit by proxy.

He'd always liked the park, and there weren't many people about by the Serpentine because the wind was cutting along that curved stretch of water. He'd stood there watching the ducks. Suddenly there was Miss Stacey, taking a lunch-hour walk with a friend. She'd been surprised to see him, and she introduced him to her friend as though he were a good acquaintance, though God knows, he'd barely said more than a few words to her in his life.

'This is Marten. He lived across the mews – and will do so again in better times,' she added, and smiled. 'Your mother told me you were coming home. What are you doing with your leave?'

'Sleeping mostly,' he'd said. It was true. Apart from two visits to the Masons' Arms with his father, and an abortive attempt to see Mary, he'd done nothing much but sleep and walk in the park.

Her friend said, 'I thought soldiers were supposed to spend their leave wildly carousing?'

'I think I'd rather sleep, or watch the ducks.' It sounded a bit bloody priggish, so he smiled and added, 'I'm sorry if I've dispelled an affectionate image of the drunken, licentious British infantryman. Perhaps I'll carouse tomorrow in the Masons' Arms.'

The friend laughed, and the cool Miss Stacey held him with her eyes. 'Don't apologise for being tired,' she said.

Then they had to go back, because the lunch hour was almost over. And as they turned away he heard the friend say she wouldn't mind him carousing with her. For the rest of the day he felt good, though he wished he could have carried on that conversation with Jean Stacey.

He was so preoccupied with his thoughts he hardly heard Lloyd's steady flow of inconsequential chatter.

'You've gone all pensive and gloomy again, Corby. You'd better tell old Lloyd what's puzzling you.'

'Love and lust. Do you keep them separate?'

'Not for long, I shouldn't think. Such a dichotomy is

for pimpled youth. I should have thought two and a half years in the war would have purged you of such adolescent nonsense.'

'The bloody war ruins a man. It's this unnatural environment. It must have arrested my normal development.'

'Yes,' Lloyd said. 'You do have a sort of naive romanticism. We could, of course, debate the question that war is an unnatural environment for man. However, too much thinking is bad for the working classes. Come on, let's get back for a spot of lunch. We fly with Hook this afternoon.'

The weather cleared up nicely before the briefing. The late autumn sunshine was quite warm as they stood in groups by the long line of machines, waiting for the major. Zac Turner pottered, checking the bomb release gear on Drinkwater's plane. It hadn't worked on the practice flight four days before, and Drink had come back with a twenty-pound bomb hanging down below the fuselage.

Zac had crashed a BE2 back in April and his multiple wounds precluded further flying. Now he was Armaments Officer for the squadron, and he was very thorough because he felt he had to work himself to death to make up for being on the ground while others flew. Lewis said Zac's internal injuries caused pressure to build up on his lower copula, and that was why he had to make hasty, spasmodic visits to a specially-designated brothel in St Pol. Lewis said the brothel had been officially sanctioned by the Wing Medical Officer, who had personally tried out all the girls to determine their suitability for dealing with Zac's complaint.

Drinkwater watched Zac adjusting a screw on the rack. Zac straightened up and stuck the screwdriver back in his pocket.

'I think it's all right. I toggled a dummy bomb with it.

It worked perfectly a dozen times.'

Drinkwater nodded. 'Thanks, Zac. If I blow up on landing you'll know that it sticks every thirteenth time.'

Major Hook stumped out on the dot, roaring at the flight sergeant to get his mechanics off their backsides. Donovan was late as usual, and got the sharp end of the major's tongue. They were ready to go and the engines were starting up all along the line, shaking the air. Donovan was strapping himself in and Marten could see his lips moving as he muttered Irish obscenities at the major's departing machine, bumping over the uneven surface of the rain-soaked field. Water splashed up from their wheels as they opened the throttles wide to lift the heavy machines off the wet, clinging earth.

It took a long time for the three flights to form up, stepped one above the other. The major liked everything just right, and this involved a lot of arm-waving and incomprehensible signals.

They crossed the front near Wytschaete and only saw two Hun machines. These fled hastily to the south-east, and who could blame them?

As this was to be the first real test of their hastily-acquired bombing skills, the major didn't hang about. He took them down low and all three flights took a turn at bombing a pathetic little transport column on the Menin - Courtrai road. They weren't very good at it because all their practice had been on bombing a whitewashed circle in a field, and with nobody firing back at them. Following Donovan down, Marten could see bombs exploding fifty yards off the road. Killer Smith did best, but only because he went so low that the bombs almost blew his tail off.

No doubt the major would evaluate the situation and make them practise some more. But what the hell? The machines weren't built for bombing, and flying that low, with an additional eighty pounds' weight, while the Hun infantry fired at him, wasn't really his kind of thing at all.

No Huns approached as they flew home. He took some deep breaths and felt the tension easing, though his jaw was aching again. The sky was a deep red along the base of the clouds. It was beautiful. He ought to try to fix it in his mind, because it might be the last good sunset he would ever see. Maybe when you were dead you just relived some small part of your life. He wouldn't mind prolonging this moment for ever. Two flights were stepped above him, fuselages and wings catching the deep glow of the setting sun. They looked like invincible fiery birds spread out across the sky. How many of them would last through the winter?

Four

LOOKING DOWN, Marten could see the big wings of the RE8 rocking in the buffeting wind. The observer in the rear seat turned his face up briefly, so he waved to him. A little encouragement cost nothing, God knows, and who'd want to ride along in one of those flying death traps?

Fast-moving winds carried them along towards the Salient. It was early morning, and the light wasn't bad. The RE8 crew would do the dirty work, flying down low to take photographs, while he and Smith and Lewis provided the cover. With a bit of luck they'd be home by nine-thirty.

Marten rubbed the lenses of his goggles. Their role was just to protect the RE8; they weren't expected to seek out the enemy. Most of the other fellows hated escort jobs, but for him it was a small relief from his nagging dilemma. Since the discussion with Lloyd, he'd felt increasingly uneasy about his reluctance to use the guns. He was no killing machine and never would be; but his moral stance led nowhere.

The pilot of the RE8 signalled, then headed north-east towards the Holthulst Forest. Lewis was worried. It was funny the way you could feel another person's unease across eighty feet of sky. But who wouldn't feel anxious with Smith leading the section? At the briefing Smith had said their job was to protect the reconnaissance machine, but not to pass up the chance of causing a little havoc if opportunities arose. Lewis had just nodded and kept quiet.

Bloody Smith was crazy. You'd think it was enough, just to do the job they were down for, stay with the Harry

Tate until the observer had got some good pictures out of the Holthulst Forest, then clear out. Smith's lust for glory would ruin them all. But he'd winked at Lewis as they followed Smith out to the machines, and just this once they had an understanding. Neither of them would willingly help Smith win a medal.

They were near the front now. Eight o'clock. Back at the airfield the other pilots would be lingering over breakfast. At home in England his father would be starting work in the wharves, and Sid Lovatt from next door would be loading up his barrow with junk furniture. Jean Stacey left her flat at eight o'clock and went to work at the pharmacy at the hospital. But he was here, with his gut in a knot, an aching jaw, and a clammy sweat under his goggles.

The first salvo of shells burst just above and to the left. The RE8 changed course slightly and lost altitude to throw the aim of the gunners, but Smith kept straight and level. Could it be that Smith had the death wish? Another cluster of shell bursts appeared on the right, closer this time, and was it too much to hope that somebody would blow Smith's head off? Lewis had dropped behind and was evading, swinging first to port then to starboard.

Ten minutes past eight. The RE8 was losing height over Staden, then turning west again. The observer had his camera set up over the side of the fuselage and had begun taking pictures of the approach to the ruined forest. This was the pilot's nightmare, holding the reconnaissance machine on a straight course while tracers scythed the air around him, and the observer frantically unloaded the camera, slid a new plate in, worked the shutter, pulled the plate out, slid in another.

Smith rolled to starboard and went down low to soften up some of the machine gunners, though it was a forlorn hope. You couldn't see them down there. The

Harry Tate flew in a direct line across the forest. God help the infantry when they tried to take it; there were hundreds of fortified positions among those shattered trees. But they'd have to try to take it sooner or later. What was it the Duke of Somewhere or Other had said? Who holds the Holthulst Forest holds Flanders.

The reconnaissance machine was hit just as it turned for another run. It reared up, then rolled over onto its back, the photographic plates fluttering out and scattering on the wind. Marten could see the observer clutching the sides of the cockpit as the aeroplane dived almost vertically at the jagged trees. Was there time, or even thought for a prayer between the stirrup and the ground? And were the two helpless men screaming louder than the wind through the bracing wires as the heavy, racing engine dragged the machine down? The orange bubble of flame preceded the dull thump of impact, and black greasy smoke drifted eastwards across the devastated forest.

He pulled his goggles up and wiped the sweat from his eyes. Smith signalled home and they turned towards the west. That was all for nothing then. Had it been worth doing, even if they'd succeeded? They all knew that the forest was crawling with Huns, that every yard would have to be fought for. What else would those fluttering photographic plates have shown?

The plane pitched, nose down, as a shell burst under the tail. God's teeth! There was just time for a frantic look back. The tail surfaces were in shreds and a severed bracing wire was lashing back in the slipstream. The machine yawed sideways. He was spinning, one wing dropping. None of the controls did what they were supposed to do.

He mustn't freeze! He must force the stiff rudder round to counter the spin, but all the pressure of his right leg moved the rudder only a fraction. Now he was spinning faster down the sky. He braced himself against the back of the seat and jammed both feet on the right rudder bar stirrup. It moved. Sweating with fear he pressed again and it moved further. He eased the control column forward and the spinning stopped. With the stick pulled back as far as he could, the shredded elevator surfaces slowly countered the dive and he opened the throttle as the plane sluggishly levelled out a hundred feet over the trenches.

Smith and Lewis were flying either side of him. He dared only fly straight and he had very little longitudinal control. The machine was bucking and pitching, and ground fire was ripping holes in his wings. Was he over the front yet? All he could hope for was to get to the British side and crash the machine.

That was Poelkapelle on the right. He had about thirty feet to spare between his wheels and the wasteland below. He'd throttled back but the churned earth was flashing beneath him faster than thought. He must shut off the fuel, pull the stick back and sink, nose up, onto the battlefield. The tail snagged and the machine smashed down into the mud, sliding and splintering, sideways into a shell hole.

He was hanging down on his seat belt. The reek of petrol made him want to vomit. It was spilling out of a hole in the gravity feed tank. Jesus! The whole machine could burn any second, but he couldn't get the belt undone because of his own sagging weight on the buckle. The shredded tail of the plane was sticking up over the rim of the shell hole and already the Huns were shooting at it. He could hear the bullets clumping through the canvas and whistling over his head.

He pulled his right foot up and braced it against the instrument panel, and still the bloody belt wouldn't undo.

His fingers fumbled with the buckle. That crackling sound was something igniting. He could smell the smoke as it filtered up beneath him, and for God's sake quick or he'd burn alive!

He'd got the buckle undone and he ripped the side of his boot as he dragged his left foot free and flung himself over the side, falling among the wing bracing wires. The smoke was thick now and the crackling turned into a roar. Heat struck him as he slid under the wires and into the deep mud of the shell hole. He sunk quickly up to his knees and wallowed towards the side of the hole, the heat burning his back through his leather coat. It was the nightmare, where you could move only very slowly away from imminent death.

The hole was big. He clung at its rim and pulled himself up over the far side. The smoke was thick, blowing in the other direction, so the Huns couldn't see what they were shooting at. He crawled to the next shell hole and slithered down into it.

The deep mud of the hole had a surface film of green slime, and the smell of sour mustard gas made him retch. He was sinking, nearly waist deep, and he dug his fingers into the wet earth near the crater's rim and hung there. Shells dropped around the hole as the Huns began pounding at the wreck of his machine. He pulled his head down and counted. They were coming over in salvos of four.

This was no longer his element. He'd forgotten how bad a wet shell hole could be, and he was shaking too much to attempt a dash to the British lines. He'd never make it, anyway. The machine guns would get him before he'd gone a dozen yards. He'd have to stay here in the hole and wait until nightfall.

There was a flash and a dull thump as the plane's main fuel tank exploded, and he huddled against the side of the hole as bits, blown high in the air, splashed down into the mud.

His wristwatch was covered with mud. He wiped the glass. It was funny the way the watch just ticked on, regardless of what happened to him. The time was eight forty-five. He must have crashed about twenty minutes ago. Now he'd got a wait of – what? – ten hours or so before darkness. But he'd got company, hadn't he. A head half-protruded out of the slime. The nose and mouth were covered and the eyes stared, unseeing, across the foul green scum.

The plane was still burning, but slowly now, and the Huns had given up shelling it, so they probably assumed he was dead. It was ten o'clock, which was ridiculous because he'd been in that hole a bloody lifetime. He had to keep dragging himself up by his fingers to keep the tops of his boots above the slime. The eyes of the nearly-submerged corpse stared from across the mud, and every few moments foul gas bubbled up and popped on the surface, quite close to the face, as if it was trying to speak.

If he put his head up somebody would probably blow it off, but he'd have to have a look round otherwise he wouldn't know which way to go when night came. Bullets zipped across the rim of the crater. So the Huns knew he was there all right, and they were waiting for him to make a move. He would just have to sit it out. It was ten-twenty. About another eight and a half hours to go.

It began to drizzle. The plane had finally burned itself out, though occasional wraiths of smoke drifted in his direction. If he got out of this alive he'd play up his damaged jaw and get himself sent home.

In that moment he heard a familiar sound, entrenching tools hacking into wet earth. Then a voice called, 'Are you all right?' So he called back that he was unhurt.

The voice called again a few minutes later. 'Stay quite

still. We'll come and get you, but it will take some time.'

'I'm not going anywhere.'

Things were looking up. It was surprising how cheerful he'd begun to feel. But his hands were still shaking.

After another twenty minutes the diggers reached him. Two infantrymen slithered into the hole through the gap they'd cut in the crater's rim. They looked like men long dead, now resurrected, bodies and faces covered clay-white. He dragged his legs out of the deep mud and groped his way round the hole towards them.

'All right, sir. Just stick behind us and keep your head down.'

The two turned back, and he followed them on his belly, crawling along the sheltered track they had dug all the way from the British line. When at last they reached the relative safety of the forward trenches it didn't seem enough just to thank the grinning, mud-caked pair. But what else could he do?

The Huns must have known what had happened and began shelling the trench out of pique. He sat crouched with the infantrymen and someone gave him a cigarette.

'These are the 4th Division trenches, sir. We're held up here because the 11th Division, over on the right, can't get into Poelkapelle. The Huns have got machine gunners in the shell holes out there. You were very lucky.'

He was cold and wet and shaking, but he hadn't got a scratch on him. 'Yes, I do seem to be lucky, don't I?'

A corpse lay under a wet groundsheet in the back of the trench. Somebody went quickly and expertly through the pockets of the dead man and found matches for his cigarette. The shells thumped down, smashing in the revetment a little farther along, and he could hear the familiar hurried shouts for stretcher bearers. 'Two dead and one wounded up here.'

There was something about the men around him that he didn't remember from the Somme and Arras. They were old veterans but they were different. They squatted, filthy and unshaven, dressed in an assortment of uniform and home-made expediencies to keep out the cold and wet. One had a sheepskin roughly round his shoulders, and another wore a leather flying coat, the lower part hacked off to give him easy movement. All had their rifles wrapped round with sacking to keep the mud out. They looked more like bandits, sullenly cynical as they glanced at him. It might have been quiet here for a while if he hadn't crashed his plane right in front of their trenches.

'Sorry to have brought this lot down on you,' he said. It wasn't much of an apology, for God's sake. Two of them might still be alive if it weren't for him.

One of them shrugged indifferently and turned away, moving off along the trench. The shelling eased. A mud-encrusted corporal indicated that Marten should follow him, and they groped along, crouching past a gap in the parapet.

'I'll take you to Company Headquarters, sir. They'll know better than I what to do with you.'

In the dug-out at the side of the old railway line a pie-eyed captain offered him a drink of brandy in a cracked, dirty mug. But then you couldn't expect gracious living up here. The captain's hand shook almost as much as his own.

He took the drink and the first mouthful warmed him. 'Bad here, isn't it?' What a bloody vacuous thing to say.

'Worse on the right.' The captain poured himself another drink and swallowed it in one gulp. 'Half a brigade lost.' He shook his head as if to clear it. 'We'd better get you out of here. You can make your way down with the wounded as far as the Casualty Clearing Station. From there you should be able to get to St Julien, then you'll be fairly safe all the way to Ypres.'

He felt guilty, walking away from it and knowing that the captain and his men had to stay there, and maybe go over the top again for the assault on the devastated forest with its bristling gun pits and pill boxes. He'd abandoned this kind of life for flying, and the assumption that killing from a distance would be slightly less distasteful. There is no limit to man's capacity for self-delusion.

It was eleven o'clock and the sun was watery through the clouds. He found the walking wounded, and six men carrying one stretcher case. Together they began the long journey. Two years ago he'd served with the infantry in this same area but couldn't recognise where he was. He'd never seen mud like this. The duckboards were treacherously coated, some of them half-submerged, and in places they disappeared. The stretcher bearers were up to their knees, trying to keep the poor sod they were carrying from sliding off into the slime. They followed the tapes, but got lost sometimes where these were broken, and the awful landscape had a sameness that confused the bearers.

Then he saw the single upjutting wall of a ruined church, its partly decapitated stone Virgin stirring his memory. Yes, there had once been a trench line – over there to the right. Fragments of it were still faintly recognisable. They'd sheltered in that trench, minds numbed by the falling shells. Then the sergeant cursing as they'd feverishly scrambled up to repel the bloody Huns. A stick grenade, fuse fizzing, arcing over and plopping in the muddy trench, and the sergeant's wild stare as he threw his body over it.

Marten paused, peering at the scene. Two years on and men were still fighting and dying for the same few acres of foul mud.

He rested for a moment longer, then followed the

others. They'd only gone a little over a mile, all of them covered clay-white with mud. They wallowed drunkenly, falling sometimes and struggled on. Unburied dead were still there from the attack of the previous week, floating in the shell holes along with the excrement and discarded equipment. He was exhausted but he ought to take a turn with the stretcher, because every time that old fellow dropped his corner the bundled shape under the groundsheet shrieked with pain. It was bloody unnerving.

They came to a battery of eighteen-pounders, up to their axles in mud, and the useless gun platforms afloat. Marten scrounged some cigarettes from the artillery officer and passed them round the stretcher bearers while they stopped for a breather.

The artillery officer said he'd crossed the easy bit and would find it really hard going when he got further back to the Steenbeke beyond Langemark. He could only assume that was supposed to be a joke.

At twelve forty-five they reached the Casualty Clearing Station up close to the railway line running out of Ypres to Thourout, and he passed round the last of the cigarettes and trudged on his own.

Pioneers had only just begun repairing the track, laying new duckboards where the old ones had sunk. When he got to the Steenbeke it was worse than he could have imagined. It had been a stream, but the shelling had smashed up the drainage system and now the stream had overflowed to a width of a hundred yards. Exhausted replacements on their way up from Ypres were wading across the icy water. You had to count your blessings in this life. At least he was going the other way. An infantryman called out and asked him what it was like farther on, and he shouted that it was marvellous, but they'd need their sun glasses and bathing drawers.

He plunged in. The water was soon over the top of his boots and Jesus, it was cold! He'd be the only pilot with trench feet. The scum of battle floated on the oily, slow-moving water. There were boots and ammunition boxes and dead transport animals drifting. And on the far side, as he waded ashore, the water's edge was littered with abandoned guns and equipment.

The going became easier. He experienced a strange feeling of freedom; he had no responsibilities until he got back to the squadron. It was like the feeling he had when he rode on a train, knowing that there was nothing expected of him until he reached his destination.

Military Police, on the look-out for deserters, eyed him suspiciously, but told him the way to St Julien, and he was able to stride on now because the road builders had been busy. The mud dried on him and began to flake off, and the sun came out for a short while, lighting up the small patches of green.

St Julien was a pounded heap of rubble. Stephen had been wounded here and was back home now, visited regularly by Mary. That thought made him pause for a moment.

A Service Corps Officer found him a mail tender going back to Ypres via Hooge, so he climbed up and held on tight as it slithered and bumped its way past the long, straggling columns of infantry. Beyond Hooge was the old front line, where they'd begun to turn this small part of Flanders into the most lethal battle in history.

The road sloped down now and ahead he could see the shattered ramparts of Ypres, and the ruined stonework of the Menin Gate, white in the pale afternoon sun. He hadn't done badly. Five hours ago he had been sitting in that wet shell hole with a half-submerged corpse for company, and the thought of waiting for nightfall for a chance to escape. Now he was rattling into Ypres, which

65

hadn't changed much, except that it was a bit more ventilated.

There was hardly a building left unscathed. Strange, the way the city was alive with men and transports, but dead at the heart. There were no civilians among the ruins. Pioneers were pulling down a wall overlooking the main road. It teetered for a few seconds then collapsed in a great heap of rubble and brick dust, shaking the ground. It was pointless to bother, the Huns would probably have knocked it down that night anyway, when they hurled their high-velocity shells into the city.

The tender drove slowly past the tumbled wreckage of the asylum building and the jagged stump of the Cloth Hall, then onto the old court house. Corps HQ was in the cellars underneath. That seemed a good place to report to. There would be a telephone and he would be able to contact the squadron.

He waited in a small cellar, made cosy with whitewashed walls and an easy chair. The thoughtful orderly had mumbled an apology and put an old newspaper on the chair so that he wouldn't dirty it with his filthy leather coat. Then a corporal brought him a mug of tea and said that the major would see him, and to take his tea with him.

He was tired and covered with mud, and his nerves were in shreds. But it was no good getting angry with the red-tabbed major just because he asked stupid questions.

'A scout pilot, you say. And you crashed – let's see – about here?' The neatly manicured finger pointed at the map showing the 4th Division position north of Poelkapelle.

'Yes, sir.'

'Interesting. What's it like up there?'

He should go and have a look, shouldn't he. 'Well, it's like a great big swamp with corpses floating in it, and it smells worse than a pigsty, and I don't think the Huns care about it enough to want to take it back from us, sir, so I suppose you could say we're winning.'

The major smiled because he'd seen chaps like this before, overwrought after a glimpse of the front.

'You Flying Corps chaps aren't used to the realities of war. It's a dirty business.' He nodded fiercely. 'A dirty business. But we won't win by being afraid of a little mud.'

There was no point in arguing. So he just said, 'No doubt you're right, sir,' and took the cigarette the major offered.

'Now you go along and telephone your unit. We can get you as far as Béthune. Major Rolls, who liaises with the Australians, is leaving in about twenty minutes. You've just got time to clean yourself up a bit.'

So he telephoned the squadron and got onto old Roper, who was pleased to hear from him because Smith hadn't seen him get out of the wrecked plane and thought he was dead. Had he remembered to take the watch and revolver from the cockpit? He said he hadn't, and Roper thought that was a pity.

He just had time to wash, and brush the worst of the mud from his clothes, and the corporal told him Major Rolls was in the car outside. 'Best not to keep him waiting, sir, he's a bit touchy.'

It was a big, mud-splashed French tourer with a canvas top. The first thing he noticed was the girl in WAAC uniform sitting behind the wheel. She was pretty. Major Rolls sat next to her, looking impatient, and bawled at him to get in the back. The car moved off. The road repairers were at work, patching up the holes made by the last bombardment. They'd got a full-time job, like those fellows who paint the Forth Bridge.

The girl missed the turning into Messines and the

major swore. She reversed, racing the engine and nervously peering back over her shoulder. She really was pretty. Then she swung the car right, past the southern ramparts of the town and over the lashed-up bridge.

The road was appalling so he couldn't rest. The car bucked and slid and the girl had to slow down because the major was swearing again. It was better beyond St Eloi. The Huns had held a salient here, all the way down to Ploegsteert, before the big push in June. Marten had counted the wrecks of six aeroplanes up till then, and these were only the ones he could see from the road. A scrap merchant could make a fortune here, just digging up aero engines. Maybe he'd do that when the war ended, get a horse and cart like Sid Lovatt, then wander around the old battlefields collecting the debris of war and turning it into something useful.

The girl must have taken the wrong turning at Wytschaete. He knew it because he could see the misty top of Mount Kemmel over on the right. If they stayed on this road they'd end up in Armentières. She was apologetic, and the major was furious. 'For Christsake! It's bad enough losing time because of the bloody roads without you going the wrong way!'

If he stuck a pin in the major, would he burst? 'I know the road, sir, because I fly over it regularly. If you let me ride in front I can navigate.'

'Very well. Let's see if we can get it right.'

So they swapped places. The major slumped into a corner in the back of the big car, pulled up his collar and dozed. And he could now talk to the girl, which seemed an altogether better arrangement. She smiled at him gratefully. Of course, he wasn't sure that he knew the road. It all looked quite different down here, but the watery sun gave an indication of where they ought to go. If he directed her south-west at Ploegsteert they'd miss

Armentières, and that was a very good idea because the bloody Huns shelled it at random intervals.

The going was very slow in places because they got caught up in the traffic to the front. They passed a huge military cemetery and the girl kept glancing sideways at the thousands of little wooden crosses. He felt he really ought to think of something to say to her, because she was already nervous enough, but it had been such a long time since he'd talked to a girl, other than those in the cafés, that he hardly knew where to begin.

'Most of them were killed back in June, so they've got used to being there now. You don't have to worry about them.'

She looked uncertain. 'I beg your pardon, sir?'

'All those dead soldiers. It's nice and peaceful for them there, you see. Nobody shells it.'

'Yes, sir,' she said, but she still looked uncertain. What more could he say? There was the unmistakable evidence of man's age-old insanity; of vast numbers slaughtered in unselfish loyalty to a jealous god, or a king, or a belief. And was that hard-bitten sergeant, or what was left of him, buried under one of those little wooden crosses? He'd posed an uncomfortable question or two, throwing himself on that grenade.

The girl frowned at a makeshift signpost and spoke softly. 'I only came out here to France a month ago. I haven't been this close to the front before. Normally I drive Major Rolls around St Pol. But sometimes I take him to Amiens or Abbeville.'

So the major doesn't get near the front often. 'Never mind, you're doing very well. And it's a bit of an adventure for you. One day you'll be able to tell your grandchildren that you were in Ypres during the battle for the Passchendaele Ridge. Of course, they won't pay any attention to you because children never listen to their elders, and anyway, you won't be able to hear their reply because one of them will have hidden your ear trumpet!'

She had a nice way of laughing softly, even though the joke wasn't very funny, and he thought it indicated a sympathetic nature.

'Do you think the war will be over before my grandchildren grow up, sir?'

'Oh yes,' he said. 'All this will be green again. We're just crossing the Belgian frontier, though you wouldn't know it. And in a year or two there will be a large fat man here, with a huge moustache and a peaked cap. He'll be asking for passports and getting nasty with people who try to smuggle out souvenirs of the battlefields.'

There was another military cemetery, with the little crosses lined up parade-ground fashion. Marten scrounged a packet of cigarettes from the girl and smoked them one after the other, trying to keep his hands from shaking. They were through Steenwerk and following the road down to Estaires. The major was now safely asleep in the back. It was beginning to get dark.

'What's your name?'

'Jean, sir.'

'Don't bother to call me "sir", I'm not particularly important. I knew a girl named Jean.'

She was slowing down, changing gear as the big car passed a column of transport wagons on the narrow road. How slim her hands were.

'Oh, I think you are important. You were shot down this morning, weren't you? That must have been terrifying. Is the Jean you know your lady friend?'

Lady friend. That was a quaint thing to say. Not wife, or lover. 'No. She just lives opposite where I used to live, before the war.'

'I think she's more to you than that, sir.'

'Why do you think so?'

'The way you said, "I knew a girl named Jean".'

'Oh, sort of women's intuition?'

'That's right.'

'Well, there's nothing romantic about it. It's just that the dustman calls at her house the same day as he calls at mine, that's all.'

Though it wasn't quite all. That morning, after he'd got across the Steenbeke, he'd found himself writing a letter to her inside his head, about how the grass had started to grow again in places, and about a stupid bird that kept singing because it hadn't got the sense to know that there was a war on, and its song seemed to match the bright green of the grass with the sun on it. Romantic rubbish of course.

It was dark now and the girl had slowed the heavy car, barely able to see the road ahead in the permitted dim glow from the side lights. They passed another column of men, trudging along in the heavy dusk towards Neuve-Chapelle.

Major Rolls woke. 'Where the hell are we, Jean?'

'Not far from Béthune, sir.'

There were flashes and the dull thump of shells bursting in the town, only a mile or so away. The Hun artillery gave it a bashing every few nights. Marten could feel the girl tensing up, but she kept on driving at the same speed. The red glow of a fire silhouetted the fretted outline of the eastern end of the town.

She turned her head briefly to the major. 'Shall I drive on, sir?'

'Yes, of course, but slowly.' The major didn't seem very happy about it and he slumped back again in his seat, huddling down inside the collar of his greatcoat.

The flashes were much nearer now, orange and yellow reflected off rising columns of smoke. It looked like dragon's breath. The girl left a gear change a bit late

71

and her movements became nervous and uneven.

'I haven't been under shell fire before.' She said it softly so that Major Rolls wouldn't overhear.

'It isn't as dangerous as it looks, and they usually stop after about twenty minutes.' Marten took another cigarette from her packet. But it was always bloody dangerous. The joy ride was over and he was back in the war again. And wouldn't it be like THEM to let him escape the smashed aeroplane only to catch a shell splinter in a Béthune side street? The match shook as he lit the cigarette. They passed a fiercely crackling building and the girl swerved sideways as a burning roof timber crashed into the street.

'Don't worry. We're through the worst of it now, and see, the shelling has eased off. The Hun gunners have done their duty and are packing up and going to bed.'

Two more shells crashed into the town, and that was the end of it.

'There,' he said. 'You did very well. I'd give you a medal if I had one on me.'

Major Rolls directed the way to Corps HQ and got out. 'Take this officer to where he can pick up a lift back to his squadron, and then collect me here in an hour.'

Marten thanked the major and directed the girl towards The Lantern, because he was sure some of the pilots would turn up there some time during the evening.

The café was filling up again now the shelling had stopped, but he found a table and ordered a bottle of champagne for them both, because he didn't want her to see him swilling down whisky. Then he noticed how pale she was, and the nervous movements of her hands as she fumbled in her bag for a tiny mirror to look at herself.

'You must think I'm a dreadful coward.' She began tidying her face with a minute handkerchief.

He didn't think that at all. 'Drink up, and in a minute or two you won't care a bit about the Huns.'

'Will they shell the town again tonight?'

She really was very attractive, in a way that crept up on you. There was a faint tinge of blue under her eyes and it gave her a palely romantic look.

'Oh no, they never shell the town twice in one night.' That was a bloody lie. 'They just like to give us all a little excitement, otherwise we'd complain we were bored.'

'Have you been out here long?'

'A fair while.'

'I'm a bit afraid all the time.'

'You'll get used to it after a while.' Another bloody lie, you never got used to it. 'And some rich, handsome Guards officer of good family will see you for the true heroine that you are. He'll kill a dragon or two, and carry you off to his crumbling castle.'

She smiled. 'I always felt sorry for the dragon in story books, so I'd rather he didn't kill one. And he doesn't have to be rich or have a big castle.'

Champagne was no good. He needed whisky to stop his hands shaking. 'All right. He won't kill the dragon, he'll make him retire and go to live in Bournemouth. Then he'll sit you on the back of his motor bike and carry you off to his semi-detached in Surbiton.'

She had been looking down at her champagne glass, and she suddenly glanced up. 'Do you have a motor bike, sir?'

She really did have the most extraordinarily attractive eyes. 'I'm afraid not,' he said softly.

'What a pity.'

And there was Lloyd pushing his way through the crowded café, with the huge Donovan close behind. The moment had passed.

Lloyd looked so pleased to see him, and pounded him on the back until he coughed and hastily put down his glass.

'We knew the Hun couldn't cope with Bloody Corby's Luck. Roper told us you were getting a lift into Béthune and I said to myself, "Where will he head for?"' Lloyd suddenly noticed the girl. 'Hello! Corby, don't be an ill-mannered bore. Introduce us to this charming young lady.'

They squeezed round the table, swilling down the rest of the champagne, and Lloyd and Donovan both talked at once, trying to get the girl's attention.

Lloyd told her about his first billet in France. 'Madame was a marvellous cook. One day a despatch rider ran over a duck right outside the cottage, and that night we had roast duck – superb!' He spread out his arms in satisfaction. 'Then we had an air raid and one of the pigs got killed, so that night we had roast pork and apple sauce – marvellous! Then her husband found a dead Hun half-buried in a field nearby, so I started eating in the mess.'

The girl's pale face flushed with laughter.

Donovan told her she ought to dine with him the next night, and said he'd fly his SE5 down to Amiens. She looked horrified, and said, what would Major Rolls think?

Then it was time for her to go, and they went with her out to the car. She pressed the starter and the huge engine roared into life. She let it idle for a moment and turned to Marten.

'I'm glad the dragon retired to Bournemouth. Perhaps I'll see you again one day?'

'And maybe I'll get a motor bike,' he said.

The car moved off.

'What was that all about?' Lloyd asked.

'Nothing.'

The tail light of the car winked away into the blackness.

'Come on.' Lloyd pulled his greatcoat collar up against the cold wind. 'Let's go home.'

74

Five

THE CAPTAIN checked his clipboard and led the pair of them along a maze of paths and roads crossing the acres of temporary huts, stores, workshops, living quarters. The depot was a vast, impersonal collecting point.

'Our problem is engines.' The captain stood aside as a lorry with a wrecked DH4 lashed to it moved slowly past them. 'There are a number of factories producing the new SE5a's, but there aren't enough engines to go round, so they have to take what they can get. Some of the new 5a's have got French-built Hispano Suiza's with imperfect reduction gear, on the principle that engines of incomplete efficiency are better than no engines at all.' He grinned at them. 'Bloody marvellous, isn't it?'

Marten supposed it was, so long as you didn't have to fly one of them.

'What sort of engines have we got?' Smith was suspicious.

'Oh, you're lucky. You've both got direct-drive Wolsey Vipers.'

Smith nodded, satisfied.

The captain took them onto the field, where the windsock hung limp. Aeroplanes, straight out from the factories, were parked in rows, lashed down in case of wind, and with groundsheets tied over the open cockpits.

'These two are yours.'

The two 5a's were different, somehow more menacing than the old SE5. Marten said so, and the captain nodded.

'Well, you've got the souped-up engine – two hundred horse power. The wing span is a bit shorter. The windscreen has been cut down, and the top decking ahead of the cockpit is deeper. You'll get damn near a hundred and forty out of it at ground level, and it will climb to ten thousand feet in eleven minutes.'

Smith had a look of hard satisfaction on his face. 'Right, we might as well go.'

Marten pulled on his helmet and goggles and fastened the seat belt. The cockpit was clean and smelled of fabric dope and fresh oil. The captain climbed onto the foot rest and held up his clipboard for him to sign for receipt of the aeroplane.

'Look after it, it's a good one.'

Marten nodded. He'd know that when he flew it.

He went through the starting procedure and held the stick well back to prevent the plane nosing over. The mechanic swung the propeller and the engine fired. He glanced across at Smith then waved to the mechanics to pull away the chocks from the wheels. The captain was standing back and shouting 'Good luck,' but he couldn't hear the words. He opened the throttle and waved his gloved hand as the machine moved forwards.

He held the nose down until he had sufficient speed then eased the stick back, lifting gently off the field. When he reached climbing speed he steepened his angle and stirred with surprise. In just over a minute he was up to eight hundred feet. It was bloody marvellous! The Viper engine was massively urgent, hauling him up faster than anything he'd flown before. He made a quick check on the instruments. Everything worked.

At two thousand feet he levelled out and circled once, waiting while Smith climbed up to join him. Smith pointed up because he wanted to see how high they could go.

At fifteen thousand feet Marten peered back over his shoulder. He could see the coast of England quite clearly, and the sharp southward turn of the French coastline at

Cape Gris Nez.

The engine was still pulling him up, but slower now. At seventeen thousand five hundred feet the old SE5 would have been wallowing, the propeller mushing in the thin air.

There was no impression of movement this far up. He and Smith seemed to be hanging in the sky. The captain had said they might get to nineteen thousand five hundred feet, so Smith would push for twenty thousand. But then Smith needed to push beyond the limits. Maybe it was because of his wife. Smith had stayed drunk for two days back in July, after the letter from his wife. She'd spent the weekend with his younger brother in a hotel in Blackpool and she thought she ought to tell him about it to square her conscience. The rumour was that she'd done this sort of thing before, and Lewis said that it was because Smith was impotent. Another one of Lewis's stories of course, but somehow it seemed devastatingly possible.

Marten felt drowsy. They'd reached nineteen thousand feet and he had to take deep breaths to get enough oxygen. They'd climbed through the alto cumulus and the sky was a clear azure infinity, unmarked except for traces of high cirrus streaking away in long curves, like the beards of Old Testament prophets.

He'd freeze to death up here. Smith was still doggedly trying to push his machine up, but they weren't going to top nineteen thousand five hundred. They were hanging on their propellers now and no amount of throttle adjustment would get them any higher. So he signalled to Smith that he was going down, and Smith nodded and held up his hand as if to say he'd given up.

The thing was to lose height slowly. Already his fingers were tingling because of the pressure changes, and he had to keep swallowing to clear his ears.

Hazebrouk was below them. Smith veered south for St

Eduarde and Marten followed him. The fine, silvery thread of the railway line stretched north-west up to St Omer and Calais. He was too high to see the train, but he could pick out the wide trail of steam from the engine hauling the carriages full of wounded, or men on leave going home. It would be weeks before he could go home on leave. But at least Peter was finally going, so he wouldn't have to worry about him for a week or two. Peter was already talking about seeing Mary. How *that* would turn out he didn't know.

The romantic fantasy of Mary, Stephen, Peter and himself being special in some way seemed increasingly insubstantial. How had he managed to cling to it for so long? On the day of the crash, during the whole of the journey from Poelkapelle, she had barely crossed his mind. Perhaps love for her had just been a habit.

But what would happen if he found himself face to face with her again? Since the war had taken over their lives, they'd all met together just once. He'd just finished his infantry training and had got leave before going to France. Peter had come home for a weekend. Stephen was about to join the army.

Mary said they were to ignore the war for that afternoon. They had a boat on the river, and he and Stephen rowed while she and Peter sat together and steered. The sun was warm and the boat moved lazily in the sluggish current.

Mary made the war seem unimportant. 'We will be as close together in fifty years as we are now.'

He'd asked, 'What will we all be?'

She placed her finger on her forehead, pretending to ponder deeply. 'Peter will go back to university and finish his BSc. Then he'll invent something that Stephen can market all over the world. You'll both become immensely rich.'

'And what about old Marten here? What will he become?' Stephen stopped rowing and rested on his oars. 'Our gloomy isolate has no interest in business or politics, no vocation for the Church or the army, no apparent mechanical aptitude, and certainly no ability as an actor if his performance in *Mrs Ford's Dilemma* is anything to judge by. God knows what we can do with you, Marten.'

Mary pouted. 'But he's so outrageously handsome.'

Stephen was continuing. 'Yes, quite. We'll agree that he's good looking in a gloomy sort of way. But what will he do with his life?'

Stephen couldn't really understand a lack of interest in business.

'I might write a book about us all,' he'd said.

Stephen leaned back and shipped his oars. 'And Mary. You haven't told us what you intend for yourself?'

She linked her arm through Peter's. 'Oh, I'll fit in somewhere.' And the boat drifted.

Smith was waving his arm and pointing down. They went into a shallow glide over the sugar beet factory and levelled out five hundred feet over the field. He circled once while Smith touched down. But it seemed a shame to land now without a quick look at the other possibilities of the new machine. So he touched the field with his wheels then opened the throttle and hauled up the nose just over the hangars. Then he climbed almost vertically to two thousand feet. It really was bloody marvellous going up like that. The Camel was more manoeuvrable, but it was tricky from all accounts and you wouldn't get a hundred and thirty plus out of it in level flight. He looped and came out into a slow roll, the weight of his body hanging on the safety belt. Now he could see dozens of small white faces looking up, so he flew low over the field and did a snap roll, because it hardly seemed fair to disappoint them.

He side-slipped down, holding the nose up as he bumped gently onto the grass, then taxied over towards the hangars and Smith's parked machine. He climbed down feeling very pleased with himself, until Major Hook bellowed at him, what the devil did he mean by doing snap rolls at zero feet over his field? The dozens of grinning faces quickly looked serious as Hook glared round and told everybody to move their backsides.

So, penitent, he handed the machine over to Duncan, who was immediately possessive about it.

'The rigger and I will give it a good going over, Mr Corby. And we'll ask Mr Turner if we can block it up on the range this evening so that you can bore sight the guns.'

'He doesn't need guns. He never fires the bloody things,' Smith said.

Sometimes Marten felt a compulsion to kick Smith.

But the next day he did fire the guns, and he shot an Albatross off Peter's tail. No denying it, his new machine had given him an edge. But God, he was tired when he got back, what with all the excitement. It had been like reaching out to grasp a shark. The whole of his machine had shuddered with the recoil of his guns, and bits had flown off the spade-shaped tail of the shark. The black-helmeted head of the pilot had jerked back, then slumped forward.

Peter walked with him to the office, rubbing the oil smudges from his face with his wet scarf.

'Thanks, Marten. I thought I was done for. That Hun was good. I just couldn't shake him off.' He paused and looked up at the rain-filled sky. 'Have you ever thought how macabre it is, that a man can die up there, all on his own, two, three miles above the earth?'

The thought had crossed his mind.

'That was very good shooting,' Peter went on. 'It's your first kill, isn't it?'

'Yes.' He wondered at the ease of it. Though it afforded him no great satisfaction that they were burying yet another airman, it had to be said that the little wooden cross planted on the grave represented one less enemy machine up there tomorrow. So was his sin so great? Smith and Drinkwater had been out there for as long as him, relishing their scores of five each.

And wouldn't you know it. Smith came into the office grinning all over his face, and he claimed an Albatross.

'Drinkwater will confirm it. I got a three-second burst into him from above and behind.' Smith splayed his squat hands to indicate his tactics. 'The weather was so thick I only got a glimpse of it going down, just north of Comines, but it was completely out of control.'

'That's two we got today,' Peter said. 'Unhappily we lost Thompson.'

Poor Thompson. What of his girl now?

'But can Drink actually confirm that your Hun crashed?' Peter asked.

'I think so.' Smith frowned. 'Who else scored today?'

'Corby claims an Albatross in the same area.'

Smith gaped. 'Corby! I thought he got that DCM of his for conserving ammunition.'

'Nope,' he said. 'I won it in a game of blackjack.'

The major came in and threw his helmet and goggles into a corner. 'Bloody lousy bombing again! This lot couldn't hit their plates with their forks. Appalling bloody display!'

Peter was trying not to smile. 'The weather was very bad, sir. But we did shoot down two Huns.'

'Oh! Who managed that on this abysmal day of failure?'

'Lieutenant Smith claims a Hun near Comines and

Lieutenant Corby shot a Hun off my tail. I didn't see Corby's Albatross crash, but I'm confident that it was out of control.'

'We'll see what Artillery say.' The major was unsmiling. 'Tea, orderly!' he bawled.

Old Roper put his head round the door. 'One of the enemy machines is already confirmed, Major. Near Wytschaete. It could be Corby's.'

Major Hook grunted, fell back into his swivel chair, and gulped noisily at his tea. 'I'm glad to hear, Corby, that your splendid detachment from the war is not altogether complete. It's about time you put that slick flying of yours to good use.' Then he turned to Peter. 'We've got a replacement in. He can take Thompson's place. Have you put in the report on those faulty reduction gears on the Hispanos?'

Now that's what Marten liked. A little appreciation. In fact he'd surprised himself, instinctively skidding down behind the Albatross and blasting it without even a split-second hesitation – like the highly efficient killing machine he was supposed to be. But he'd done it for Peter. Was that why he felt no guilt?

He went back to his hut. God, he was worn out. Lloyd was examining some unfamiliar baggage stacked on the spare bed. Thompson's belongings were still as he'd left them.

'You got an Albatross then?'

'Yes. I had to shoot it off Peter's tail.'

'Why do you feel you have to qualify your reply?'

'Did I? I didn't mean to.' He glanced across at the pile of baggage. 'Thompson's replacement.'

'Yes.' Lloyd was examining the tag on the handle of the largest case. 'Quick off the mark, aren't they? Thompson went down this morning and his replacement had already arrived.'

'We were one short already. They were bound to send somebody in. Has anybody heard what happened to Thompson?'

'Roper tells me the lad's in hospital at Merville. Fractured skull. But he'll be all right.'

'Good that he's still alive. We'll have to go through his things before Bates packs them. Maybe we should visit him?'

'Yes. Maybe we should.'

But they probably wouldn't. He'd said that to Lloyd when the last fellow to use that bed had crashed. What the hell was the chap's name? He'd quite forgotten.

Lloyd said, 'Do you ever wonder at the monstrous efficiency of the logistical machine? Here's the baggage of Thompson's replacement, and no doubt some young fellow is on the boat now, heading for the depot, ready to replace the replacement. And back in England there's yet another young fellow making his first solo flight, and already earmarked to replace him, or me.'

'Oh, come now! Nobody can replace you.' It wasn't like old Lloyd to be so pessimistic. What had got into him? 'You and I are indestructible.' He touched wood.

'You maybe, with your luck.' Lloyd looked up from the name tag on the bag he was examining. 'For God's sake! This fellow is a Yank. It says here, "Second Lieutenant William Sheridan Harvey". Only a bloody Yank would have a name like that. And see here, on the side of this bag, there's a label. "SS Northern Star. Boston, USA." Now what do you make of that?'

'So he's an American.' He lifted his head off the pillow. 'There are, after all, a lot of them in the Flying Corps.'

'Why couldn't he have joined his own Air Service? I don't know what this squadron is coming to. We've got colonial riff-raff, a crazy Irishman, a doom-ridden poker player from North Paddington. And now an impetuous American.'

A short, slim young man in a well-tailored uniform appeared in the doorway. His eyes were quite expressionless as he glanced at Lloyd examining his bags. Lloyd, shameless, continued to search for labels.

'Hello. You're Harvey, I take it. I was trying to work out where you come from. Do come in, old chap, and close the door. These huts are miserably cold.'

Harvey smiled slowly and closed the door. 'Hi there. I'm Harvey, from Wyoming. That's in the far West.' He had a pleasing slow drawl.

'Far west of what?' Lloyd had assumed his innocent expression.

Harvey thought for a moment, as though taking Lloyd's question seriously. 'Well, it's not so much a precise geographical location, because the Pacific states beyond the Rockies are even farther west. It's more of an indication of a way of life. And I suppose it could be said that it helps to identify you, culturally speaking, in the same way that if you said you came from Wigan it might provide me with a preliminary, rough and ready-made guide to the kind of person you are.'

Lloyd looked dumbfounded. Then he blinked and said, 'I say, Corby, I think this chap will fit in quite well.'

Marten grinned at Harvey and got up off his bed. 'I'd better introduce you. This is Lieutenant Lloyd, but he isn't from Wigan, he's from Cheltenham Spa, and that ought to tell you quite a lot about him. And I'm Corby, from Paddington in London, which is, culturally speaking, far west of Chelsea.'

Harvey nodded and smiled with his eyes, though the rest of his face remained impassive. He was at least a head shorter than Lloyd. But though he was slim he was wiry, and there was about him an indefinable impression of contained energy. His grip was powerful when he shook hands.

Harvey produced a packet of American cigarettes and handed them round. 'What's the war like here?'

'It could be worse,' Marten said, because there was no point in alarming a newcomer. 'Just lately we spend much of our time supporting the infantry in the Ypres sector.'

'Hell now! And I thought I'd be clawing the Huns down out of the sky.'

'Oh, we do some of that as well,' Lloyd said. 'We'll start breaking you in tomorrow. Tonight you can come to a little party in the mess. Captain Peter West has just got his MC through, and he goes on leave tomorrow.'

'Great.' Harvey began to unpack.

Then an orderly from the squadron office looked in with the message that Major Hook would be obliged if Lieutenant Corby would report immediately.

'That means move your backside,' Lloyd said.

He moved, straightening his cap as he approached the admin buildings. What could it be about? The major hadn't sent for him in weeks.

The major was seated behind his desk, and he looked weary.

'Sit down, Corby.' He stared down at the message form in front of him, then glanced up. 'Did you see Smith on your way over?'

He said he hadn't.

The major looked impatient. 'Well, we'll get started without him.' He lit a cigarette. 'Because of the poor weather, ours was the only squadron of SE5's operating in the area just south-east of Ypres this morning. Artillery report seeing an SE5 shooting down an Albatross.'

The major blew smoke up at the ceiling then looked back at the message form and read from it. 'A pale blue Albatross DV was found on its back, almost intact, on farm land at Lindenhoek, south-west of Wytschaete. The pilot was found to be dead, and a superficial examination of the body indicated that he was killed by a bullet entering his back and passing out through his chest. The personal papers found on the body identify the pilot as Hauptmann Josef Steiner.'

God Almighty! Steiner dead! It didn't seem possible.

Major Hook put down the form and sighed, rubbing his jaw with his hand. 'So now we have a problem.'

Smith knocked and looked round the door.

'Come in, Smith, and sit down. It seems that either you or Corby has shot down Steiner. A crashed Albatross has been found near Wytschaete. Steiner was still in his cockpit, and very dead with a bullet through his back.'

Smith gaped and sat down slowly.

The major went on, 'You've each claimed an Albatross in the same area, but only one machine has been found. You each report firing a burst through the rear of a Hun, and clearly Steiner was shot from behind.'

Smith cut in. 'Sir. It *must* be mine! I fired at close range and saw my Hun slump over in the cockpit as he went out of control.' He paused, as if shocked.

Smith really wanted that kill badly. It would put him in the big league. And Smith turned to him and said, 'It *couldn't* be yours, Corby, could it?'

'Why the hell not!'

Major Hook crushed out his cigarette and lit another one. 'Neither of you can say for sure, on the evidence that we have at this moment, that you killed Steiner. We've all of us pretended to be out of control to get a Hun off our back, and they, of course, do the same. The weather was bad. Either of you could have *thought* your Hun had crashed. One of them clearly didn't, but got away in the mist. If this had been any old Hun it wouldn't matter. But Steiner! Now we'll have Wing, Group – perhaps even

Army Headquarters involved.' He sighed. 'I do not enjoy notoriety, gentlemen. It invariably means visits from our masters, and that I can do without. And it invariably means a lot of paper work, and I can do without that as well. Now you'd better go, the pair of you, and leave me to it.'

'Oh, and Corby,' he called, as they both started for the door. 'This would be your first kill, wouldn't it?'

'Yes, sir.'

'Well, let's hope that it's a precursor.'

But you'd have thought the major could have been a bit happier about it. After all, Steiner had been a scourge. He'd claimed eighteen British machines in August alone.

The news was all around the camp in half an hour, and Marten was just a bit taken aback the way everybody assumed that it was Smith who'd shot Steiner down. It was only to be expected, of course. Smith was popular and aggressive. And he was already recounting, with some embellishments to the story, the way he'd outfought the great ace. But it couldn't be Smith's kill, could it?

Marten was late for dinner in the mess because the chat with the major had put him behind in his schedule. He liked to check his own guns and sort out any problems with Duncan before finishing for the day. So by the time he got to the mess nearly everybody was seated.

He'd made the mistake of looking at the board to see what was projected for the next day. He was down for the early patrol and Drinkwater was leading the flight. There was no way of winning. Either you looked at the board before dinner, and then you couldn't eat because you were down for something nasty the next morning. Or you put off looking at the board and spent the entire meal worrying about what it might have in store for you. And he was worried now because Drink as a flight commander was an unknown quantity. Maybe Drink would feel he had to prove his newly acquired responsibility and win the war, with his flight right behind him.

The only empty space he could see was between Lewis and Baker, the Canadian. Preoccupied with the possibility of disaster with Drinkwater in the morning, he barely heard what Lewis was saying. Not that it mattered very much, because Lewis talked non-stop without looking up from his plate.

The orderlies served champagne, supplied by Peter as a parting gesture before going on his leave. It contrasted nicely with the overdone meat pie. You'd think the cooks were paid agents of the Kaiser.

Once he'd drunk some champagne he began to feel better. He reckoned he might as well make an effort to listen to Lewis because the meal was going to drag on a bit. It was Lewis's day for grand strategy and he was explaining how the war had begun because of railway timetables.

Baker looked confused. 'But I thought it was because some Serbian guy shot an Austrian prince?'

'He wasn't a prince, he was a bloody archduke.' Lewis waved his forkful of meat pie. 'What is the point in trying to hold an intelligent conversation with a Canadian backwoodsman who doesn't know his axe from his elbow?'

Baker was interested now. 'No, go on. What's this about railway timetables?'

Lewis put down his fork and assumed his pedantic pose. 'No country in Europe had a standing army large enough to fight a full-scale war. So any plans for war necessitated the mobilisation of reservists. In turn, mobilisation of reservists requires the use of railways. The French had to mobilise three and a half million reservists in a week, so you can imagine the problems, and you can see why the railways demand very tight timetabling. Now railway timetables take months to prepare and allow no room for manoeuvre. When the Czar, who had no real intention of going to war, tentatively ordered the mobilisation of the Russian army, the Kaiser felt impelled to do the same. But this made war inevitable because in the German mobilisation plans, the railways were timetabled to take the army right into Belgium. No diplomatic improvisation was possible because it would have made a cock-up of the whole schedule. The German statesmen and generals had only minimal control over the following events.'

Lewis smiled triumphantly, and Baker narrowed his eyes because he was sure there must be flaws in the theory but he wasn't fast enough to think of them.

Baker put down his fork and knife. 'You're saying that nobody really meant the war to start. But that's nonsense. All the countries of Europe had been preparing for war for years; stockpiling arms, building battleships, making plans.'

Lewis shook his head. 'The plans and the armaments were always intended as deterrents. So also was the call-up of reservists. The machinery of mobilisation ran away with them. They were trapped by their own logistics. So you see, the destiny of Europe was decided by railway timetables.'

It was a bit too slick. It absolved everybody from blame. So Marten said, 'It was nobody's fault, then — nobody need feel guilty about the millions of dead?'

Lewis shook his head again. 'Ultimately, no. We are all of us, from generals down to privates, carried along by the momentum of circumstance.'

'But decisions were made. People chose to do one thing or another.'

Lewis was warming to his subject. 'No. In the first place your range of choices is really very limited. Most of the time circumstances dictate your actions. And in the second place, when choices seem available to you, you react in a certain way because you have been conditioned by all the previous circumstances of your life. You may think that you have a free choice, but it is an illusion.'

'Not so!' You had to be drunk to pursue an argument like this one. 'If that were true, and if I had access to all your previous experience, I would be able to predict your behaviour.'

'Certainly.'

It sounded very simple and rational, but he didn't think Lewis could be right. You can condition men, even turn them into efficient killing machines; but in the end some will choose to behave illogically. Like the sergeant who'd made that split-second decision to save his fellows by throwing himself on the grenade. Man was as much the product of his choices and couldn't ultimately evade responsibility for his actions.

And what of his own choice to stay out here despite his jaw wound? Lewis would say he was conditioned, by patriotism, and loyalty to Peter and the others. But until today he'd evaded the consequent responsibilities. It made no real sense.

Old Roper called for silence for the major. And the major, who didn't often dine in the mess, stood up and thanked Peter for all he'd done, and congratulated him on the way he'd managed to get his Military Cross to coincide with his leave. Then he asked them all to drink to Peter, which they did. They gave him three hearty cheers and a monogrammed cigarette case.

Peter rose to his feet. It was that smile of his which trapped you. His sincerity gave you no room for manoeuvre.

'Thank you all. I'm sorry to be leaving you at this difficult time, but I've been out here so long now that nothing short of the Kaiser's appearance in this mess could delay my leave further.'

Smith shouted, 'We'll have his balls if he shows up here.'

Peter smiled patiently. 'I don't expect to find such good masculine company back in England, but the company I seek will certainly be more attractive.'

They all cheered loudly and thumped the table.

'I leave my flight to Lieutenant Drinkwater, confident that he could lead no finer band of drunks and ne'er-do-wells. They may not be able to find their way to the Salient on their own, in fact one of them cannot even find his way to the latrine without a large-scale map, but they are a good bunch.' He stopped and shrugged, and grinned hopelessly. 'I'll miss you all. I'll be back in a few weeks.'

They all thumped the table again. What a splendid fellow he was! And he'd bought them enough champagne to float a battleship. Rumour had it that Major Hook would be going to Wing HQ next month, and Peter would take command of the squadron on his return from leave. At least that would put Peter behind a desk for much of the time, so he wouldn't have to worry about him so frequently.

Major Hook and old Roper stayed a while longer then left, and the serious drinking began. Drinkwater called for a toast to Hauptmann Josef Steiner, and they all drank very solemnly, though not without a feeling of relief that the scourge of the Ypres sector had passed over into the Great Beyond. But Drink, who seemed genuinely moved by the death of the ace, then proposed a toast to Smith, which was a bit off because he was thus implying that Smith had definitely shot Steiner down. Smith looked mighty pleased with himself, though just a little embarrassed as he glanced up the table to where *he* was sitting.

Benge punished the piano, and Zac Turner sang *She*

was poor but she was honest with a powerful cockney whine, and they all joined in the choruses. If you were drunk enough it was hilarious. Who'd have thought of rhyming 'crime' with 'shime'?

Marten couldn't help wondering what the American, Harvey, thought about it all. It was a bit of a madhouse, what with Baker standing on his hands, and Donovan trying to pour beer into his upturned mouth. Harvey's face remained impassive but his eyes registered amusement.

The noise was getting excessive. He'd waited for the moment, and now he would buy Peter a last drink and have a little chat. So he went to the bar and called for two whiskies.

'Have you got hold of them, Mr Corby?' And because he knew his gentlemen, the barman kept his fingers round the glasses.

'Yep.' He was swaying a bit. 'Now just steer me in the direction of Captain West.'

Peter smiled but shook his head reprovingly. 'Marten, you should go easy on that stuff. You've got to fly early tomorrow.'

'Don't worry, don't worry. Last one. Just to drink to your leave.'

Peter was a bit stoned as well. You could tell by the slightly glazed look in his eyes as he reached out to take the glass, and almost missed it. 'Thanks, Marten.' He took a deep breath and straightened himself up, trying to concentrate his thoughts.

'Marten.'

So now would follow a little homily.

'Yes, Peter.'

Peter fumbled and took out a cigarette. He held it to his lips, then forgot it, frowned, and slowly lowered his hand. 'You've seen more of the war than most of us. But you remain staggeringly innocent.' He raised the unlit cigarette to his lips, then forgot it again. 'You want to hang onto that.'

He flicked his lighter and held it out, but Peter didn't seem to notice.

Peter frowned very hard. 'I suppose it's because I've drunk too much, but I keep thinking that there's something I ought to say to you. Something important.'

'It'll keep.'

But Peter shook his head, still frowning. 'Something important, but I can't think what it is. All the time we've been friends, everything has gone my way.'

'We all get pretty much what we deserve,' Marten said, a generalisation with some truth in it. And he tried again to light Peter's cigarette.

'You always wanted Mary, didn't you?'

'Yes,' he said. 'But it doesn't matter now.' He meant it, because it really didn't matter all that much any more.

'You're a good friend, Marten. And you saved me today.'

'I still owe you,' he said, because for God's sake, you didn't find many people like Peter in this life.

Peter stubbed out the unlit cigarette. 'There's the possibility of a job for me back home, at the Central Flying School.'

'You ought to jump at it. Mary would be pleased. You and she could pick up the threads again. You'd have time.'

Peter stopped frowning, as if he'd made a decision. 'No, I'll be back, with you, Killer, Drink and the rest. We've still got to win the war. You'll take care while I'm gone? And keep looking behind you.'

'Yes. Don't worry about me. I'll be all right. Corby's luck.'

Peter looked at him, then shook his head, still smiling wryly. 'A broken jaw, your nerves in tatters, drinking too much, and you still believe in Corby's luck.'

'Yes,' he said. 'I am lucky.'

'Or staggeringly innocent.' Peter held out his hand. 'Right then. I'm going now because I've drunk too much and I've got to leave at five tomorrow.'

'Right then,' he said, and he gripped Peter's hand. There was, after all, some truth in all that band-of-brothers rubbish.

There was a lull in the horseplay while Peter said all his goodbyes. The Killer seemed moved as he pumped Peter's hand. Nobody could remember what it was like, not to have Peter there with them.

And Marten felt quite lost after Peter left. Then Smith started to haul himself up on a roof beam. The thing to do was take refuge up in a corner of the small bar. Harvey and Lloyd joined him.

'God's teeth! I thought the British were supposed to be a quiet, reserved people,' Harvey said, gaping incredulously as Smith began swinging himself from beam to beam while the others threw cushions and rolled-up newspapers at him. 'Is it like this every night in here?'

'Oh no,' Lloyd said. 'It's rather quiet tonight.'

He felt a bit embarrassed, seeing the scene through Harvey's eyes. For God's sake, they did look like a bunch of imbeciles. And why didn't the bloody bar staff clear away the empty glasses? You couldn't move an elbow without knocking one over. Lewis had fallen over a chair and was having difficulty in getting up, the drunken sod. He'd get up and help him, but each time he moved the bar seemed to spin around. Templer, always a perfect gentleman, was hauling Lewis to his feet, and Bengy was trying to hold him steady.

There were loud cheers because Smith had managed to swing the whole length of the hut. You had to hand it to Smith. He was the only man in the squadron who could do that. Mind you, a well-trained performing ape could manage it. And Smith didn't look very well. He'd gone a funny green colour and was heading for the door.

The atmosphere was very thick, what with all the cigarette smoke. Donovan had the right idea though, he'd just put his elbow through a window, and now he was bawling out to Smith not to throw up on the major's vegetable patch. It was bloody funny.

The singing had got a bit ragged but Benge and Zac Turner got through six more verses of *The Bold Aviator*. How the hell did Captain Carver manage to sing without taking the cigarette from his lips? Jesus H Christ! What a din!

Lloyd had dragged him to his feet to join in the toast. They sang it together in frightful chorus.

'We meet 'neath the sounding rafters
The walls all round us are bare,
They echo the peals of laughter;
It seems that the dead are there.'

Sleep. That's what he needed. So he pointed to the door and Lloyd and Harvey stumbled out after him.

It was a marvellous night. There was a star up there for everybody. They paused for breath in the clean air.

'So stand by your glasses steady
This world is a world of lies.
Here's a toast to the dead already,
Hurrah for the next man who dies.'

It was odd how sad that sound was, carried away and lost against the immensity of the starred night.

Over in the hangars the mechanics were still working, patching up the planes ready for the morning. Behind the sounds of clattering tools, and the laughter from the mess, they could hear the spasmodic, far-off thump of the guns at the front.

Harvey was quiet, watching the eastern horizon, strangely lit every few seconds by the distant flashes.

'That's where it's all happening?'

'Yes. We sleep, safely peripheral to it all.'

'Do I go over there tomorrow?'

'I shouldn't think so. Not for a day or two.'

They walked through the small copse which Marten had always thought of as a sort of sanctuary. If God existed He'd put up those trees there to remind Himself that there was some purpose to His creation, here in Northern France.

They reached the hut and Lloyd blundered into the doorpost. Harvey lurched in and fell full length onto his bed, muttering into his pillow, 'This is a damned funny way to enter a war.'

Lloyd switched on a torch and stood it on the table. Then he sat and began pulling his boots off.

'You'll get used to it in a day or two. No standing on ceremony here. All bloody informal. I'll take you over to the office tomorrow and we'll find out what machine you've got.' He yanked off the other boot and flung it into the corner. 'Of course, the major has his funny little ways, but we could do a lot worse.' Lloyd talked on quietly, almost to himself, as he undressed, then fell into bed and was instantly asleep.

Marten washed his face and drank some water. He'd feel a bit thick in the morning but it would clear as soon as he got into the air. He turned to Harvey who was still flat on his face, fully dressed and snoring softly. If only he could do that, just fall sound asleep. He pulled the boots off the sleeping Harvey and threw a blanket over him.

His nerves felt a bit jangled, and his jaw ached now that he was in bed. It had been quite an eventful day, what with shooting that Hun down. And then the party for Peter. He didn't want to think about the morning patrol, with Drinkwater leading, so he thought about Peter going on leave, and Mary waiting for the boat train at Charing

Cross. Was she awake at that moment, turning in her bed, happy at the thought of Peter coming home? Or was she still worried about herself and Peter being different?

A funny thing was, he just couldn't think about Mary in physical terms. He'd tried sometimes, imagining her with no clothes on, but the thought always tailed off into something else. Yet he couldn't think about Jean Stacey for long without recalling her long legs, and the way her hips moved as she walked. But that wasn't all. There was something else about her that made him restless and disturbed his sleep.

He dozed fitfully, and awoke suddenly sweating from the dream of the burning cockpit. It was still dark. His watch said two-thirty. Then he fell asleep again, and he was on the boat train entering Charing Cross. He knew it was only a dream, but he kept looking for Jean Stacey. She wasn't there.

Six

HE TURNED back towards the hut, scuffing the cinders with
his boots. There was no denying that he was a bit upset
the way Smith had been credited with the killing of
Steiner. It wasn't so much that he wanted that kind of
recognition. What offended him was the way the two hot-
shot officers from Group had half listened to his version
whilst passing his and Smith's service records between
them. What the hell had records of their previous service
got to do with it?

Then Smith just accepting the credit that way, as if it
was his rightful due! No word of regret. Just a grin of
triumph. So he'd be blowed if he was going to attend the
parade for the war photographer. He had no intention of
going down in history standing behind a grinning Smith.

Harvey, pale with excitement, followed him into the
hut a few minutes later.

'It screwed up, you say?' Lloyd smiled at him.

'Yeah. Screwed up like a broken kite. 'Course,
Drinkwater and Donovan did all the real work, but I think
I put a couple of bullets through that two-seater's wing.
And Drink is giving me a third share in the kill.' Harvey
grinned, suddenly embarrassed by his own loss of
composure. 'Oh, I realise that this is pretty run-of-the-mill
stuff to you two. But wait till the folks back home
in Wyoming hear about it! I'll have my picture in the
Casper *Sentinel*.' He turned the whole thing into a joke,
splaying out his hands to indicate the newspaper headline.
'PROFLIGATE SON OF PROMINENT CASPER LAWYER MAKES GOOD IN
WAR WITH HUN!'

Lloyd blinked. 'Casper! There's no such place. You've

just made that up.'

'High Plains country,' Harvey said. 'On the North Platte River.'

'Did you hear that, Corby? You've got to admit it. Just being in Harvey's company is an education.' Then Lloyd noticed him frowning. 'Corby, you are a gloomy sod. What is the matter with you?'

'I've just heard that Smith is getting the credit for shooting down Steiner. Two officers from Group are over in the major's office now. It seems the field marshal himself got interested. And because the story is in all the newspapers back home, the brass have decided that a clear-cut decision must be made. So they've come out in favour of Smith. We're all to have our photograph taken, grouped round Smith, some time this afternoon.'

Lloyd nodded. 'Well, you might have made the same decision in their place. Admit it now.'

'I admit it. But Smith must know that his claim is doubtful. I actually saw my Hun hit the ground.'

Lloyd slapped him on the back. 'Cheer up. You don't care that much, do you? But you know that Smith needs that kind of recognition. He'd swap his mother for the Military Cross, and his wife for a long-service medal.'

He shrugged. Of course Lloyd was right. If Smith wanted fame that badly, then maybe he should feel sorry for him. But he still felt sour.

Lloyd had started to pull on his flying clothes because B Flight was on the mid-morning patrol. Pausing as he dragged his scarf round his neck, he said, 'Tell you what. You, me and Harvey will go out tonight and have a civilised dinner. Now what do you say? And after that we could go to The Lantern and see . . . ' He cupped his hands on his chest. 'Right? Good. See you both later.' He clumped out in his heavy flying boots.

That was one thing he liked about old Lloyd. When

you were feeling down he always gave you support.

Harvey was still keyed up, so he took him for a walk, into St Eduarde. They found the small estaminet open. Madame cooked them bacon and eggs. Harvey talked about his family.

'My grandpa fought in the Civil War. He was separated from the Union Army just after the war ended, and he got on a train, back to Chicago, Illinois. That was his home town. But half-way home the Great American Dream got him, and he went out West instead. He panned for gold in the Black Hills, and he shot buffalo to feed the railway workers. Then he met my grandmother and they settled in Wyoming.'

'Is he still alive?'

'Sure he is. Very spry for his age.' Harvey winked.

They walked back to the airfield, and on the way he told Harvey about life in the mews, and about himself and Peter going to school together. They waited at the edge of the field because he could see the small dots on the horizon as B Flight came back.

After a moment he was able to count them. There was somebody missing.

Carver looked done in as he walked over from his machine.

'Sorry, Corby. I'm afraid Lloyd went down.'

'Yes,' he said in shock.

Carver pulled off his helmet and all the grey hairs showed. 'Probably some structural damage picked up in the scrap.' He frowned. 'We were well over our side, and he signalled that something was wrong. Then he suddenly went into a dive and crashed into the Nieppe Forest. His machine broke up as it hit the trees.'

'I see,' he said. Well, it could happen to anybody. A control wire suddenly parts. A gasket blows. A bracing wire snaps. Some small damage to the airframe, unnoticed by a weary mechanic, and a wing folds up.

'I'll tell Roper to start phoning around,' Carver said.

'That's right.' He took a deep breath. 'Old Lloyd's probably trying to get a lift back, busted compass in one hand and a French-English dictionary in the other.'

Carver looked at him steadily for a moment. 'Could be,' he said. But he didn't look as if he believed it. 'We'll know later.'

He just stood there, not knowing what to do. Harvey said something but he couldn't take it in. Harvey stayed for a moment then tactfully left him to it.

He walked back to the hut and sat on his bed. The hut was still untidy, the way Lloyd had left it. Why should he be surprised that Lloyd had gone down? After all, Lloyd hadn't been a very good pilot. The wonder was that Lloyd had survived this long. But they had been together in that hut for months. Four replacements had come and gone, using that third bed, while he and Lloyd had argued, played cards, got drunk, attended funerals, and looked for girls in Béthune and St Pol.

He groped for the flask in the locker and took a long swallow. Lloyd had said, only a day or two ago, that some young replacement was probably in the Pool right then, ready to fill his place.

Then he noticed the letter on his locker. Bates must have put it there while he was out. It was from Mary. He carefully slit the flap and took out the heavy, expensive paper.

> *'Quants Farm*
> *Playdon*
> *Rye*
> *Sussex*
> *6th November 1917*

My dear Marten,

> *As you can see from this address, Peter and*

I have left the sinful city for innocent Sussex. We are staying at Roger's farm, so we are suitably chaperoned. The weather remains generally foul, but I do not mind. Peter and I take long walks on the shingle and I pretend to be knowledgeable about tides and sea birds.

I met Peter off the boat train. I was nervously anxious in case I should miss him in the thousands of servicemen, and when I finally saw him walking towards me I was so proud of him, yet stiff with alarm in case he had changed, or I had changed in my feelings towards him. You see, you don't know until you actually talk to somebody. But then I saw how tired he looked and was suddenly ashamed of all my selfish doubts.

Happily Peter is now rested and quite relaxed again. It is so delightfully peaceful here and he is most reluctant to return to London, so I suppose we shall stay on here for a few more days.

Dear Marten. You are the only person to whom I could extend such a confidence. Peter has asked me to marry him whilst he is on leave.'

He carefully put the lid on the flask and slid it back into the drawer.

'I was so very grateful that he should propose, but I did not know how to reply. I want him, but I want him here, with me, safely in England. I feel that after his extensive flying service in France, there should be no reason for him to reject the offer of a posting to the Central Flying School. Experienced pilots are needed for

the training programme, and if we are to be married, that would be his best course. Peter is rather reticent about this. I suppose I should say that I will marry him even if he returns to France. But Marten, I know so many war widows, and I do not think I could face such a prospect. However, at this moment I float on a cloud of romantic euphoria, confident in my ability to persuade him that he has done his fair share of service at the front.

Please write soon. Peter tells me that you saved his life. Knowing you as I do, I am sure any expressions of my gratitude would make you creak with embarrassment. But I know that it is not necessary for me to explain my feelings to you. You always understood me far too well.

I miss you. Do take great care of yourself. You are often in my thoughts. And I have not yet forgiven you for allowing your handsome jaw to be broken in heaven knows what heroic encounter.

Yours affectionately,
Mary '

He carefully folded the letter and put it back in the envelope. Mary was, after all, just a human being. She was lonely and insecure because the war had dragged on for too long, and killed her cousin, and taken her brother and all her friends from her. What would happen now? If Peter came back here, that could be the end of it. Their relationship was under too much stress when they were separated.

But he couldn't bring himself to care right then, because he was too sad about old Lloyd. He'd care tomorrow perhaps.

Smith briefed him and Harvey for an escort job. It had to be important because a major was flying as observer in the Ak W. Just before they left Smith looked serious and told him how sorry he was about Lloyd. But he didn't feel like replying.

Smith led, with Harvey on the left and him on the right. Over the Nieppe Forest he peered down. Lloyd's plane was there somewhere, along with a dozen more, probably. At St Claire they picked up the Ak W, then positioned themselves over it like protective hens as they crossed the front at eight thousand feet.

Some shells burst quite close, but he felt numb, almost indifferent, though maybe the whisky he'd drunk had something to do with that. Then they went down lower and the observer on the Ak W started his work. There was no thought for anything now but Huns.

He could see the observer peering over the side of the fuselage. He wasn't taking any pictures, just looking.

They followed the Courtrai-Menin road, and then went in a wide loop, all the way up to Ingelmunster, then west to Roulers. Apart from anti-aircraft fire nothing untoward happened, until they turned back, climbing and approaching the near side of the Passchendaele Ridge.

He was thumping his knee with his gloved hand, trying to get it warm. A small dark shape passed between two clouds. He waved to Smith and banked to port, searching, and Smith and Harvey joined him because they were over their own side now and the Ak W was safe.

They headed for the large gap in the clouds and the dark shape appeared again briefly. It was an LVG two-seater. They were good for bait, but not usually over the British side. He looked quickly round the sky, just in case, but cloud enveloped them again. As it thinned and they flew into another clear patch, the LVG was directly in front of them.

Smith waved that it was his and dropped down, coming up again under its tail. And the Hun observer was dragging his Parabellum gun round and trying to depress the barrel to get a shot at him. Smith fired, and almost immediately both his guns jammed. It was very satisfying to see Smith with a problem. The Hun pilot had swung his machine round to give his observer a field of fire and tracers were flicking round Smith. Smith was thumping the cocking handle of his Vickers gun, trying to clear it, but he was staying right behind the LVG.

Harvey tried an oblique shot then pulled up over the top of the Hun machine, which was a stupid thing to do. He'd have to tell him about that later. The Hun observer managed to place a few rounds through Harvey's tail before dragging the gun round for another burst at Smith. And still Smith wouldn't get out of the way and give somebody else a chance.

Marten flew up under the Hun's tail, almost touching wings with Smith, and on the turn he got the LVG in his Aldis sight and raked it from nose to tail. The black-crossed machine fell sideways and steeply down. The pilot's head was slumped forward and the observer was leaning out over him, trying to pull him back off the stick.

The LVG was a black spot diminishing. He watched it falling down the chasm between banks of drifting cloud. Down, burning now, to the five miles of devastation where the front had been pushed eastwards. Now it spiralled, a tiny blazing speck, plunging into the huge and unnatural corruption. There was a small bubble of flame, then black smoke.

That was for poor old Lloyd. And he felt nothing but a sour pleasure at cheating Smith of his prey. Let Smith try and claim that one.

But Smith was nowhere to be seen. Harvey was circling and waving to him. They looked for Smith for several minutes, but with cloud thickening at that altitude, they weren't likely to find him. So he signalled to Harvey and they went down, following the south side of the low ridge stretching westward as far as Cassel. The quiet countryside was gold where the wide shafts of late afternoon sun pierced the clouds.

Their shadows leaped up at them as they skimmed low, easing their wings over treetops and small hamlets, untouched by the war since the autumn of 1914.

They flew low over the forest once more, but he didn't look for Lloyd's machine. It did no good. He felt bitter, and that did no good either.

Ahead was the long straight road cutting through the south of the forest, obliquely down to Haverskerque. He waved to Harvey and pointed to the big open motor car with the motor cycle escort. There was a pennant on the car and the occupants of the back seat had red staff bands on their caps.

Marten flew low over the car and hauled up his right wing, climbing and turning to come round behind it again. Anxious faces peered back at him from the car as he closed on it, touching the road with his wheels. The motor cyclist swung sideways and the car bounced onto the grass verge as he lifted the plane just over it and touched the road again before hauling up and climbing once more. Glancing back, he could see angry, frightened faces and a staff officer brandishing a revolver.

He felt better.

But Major Hook wasn't in the least bit amused and sent for him that evening before dinner.

'For Christ's sake! What do you think you are about?'

Marten stood to attention and kept his eyes on a small spider crawling up the wall behind the major's old swivel chair.

'Why didn't you return with Captain Smith? You strafed Brigadier General Payne's car and one of his aides got your machine number. He's been onto Wing demanding a full report on what action I'm taking.' Hook glared up at him. 'I ordered all C Flight pilots to report for the photographer because of this bloody Steiner affair. Dammit, that was an official parade, but you didn't attend. Have you decided to detach yourself entirely from the rest of us?'

It was no good repeating the lie that the message hadn't reached him. Anyway, he didn't really want to lie to the major.

Hook sighed and leaned forward, scooping up his service record, still in his tray since the morning session with the two officers from Group.

'You've got an odd history, Corby. Working class background – not that I hold that against you. Grammar school. Lance corporal in the East Surrey Regiment. Wounded in the Arras battles. DCM.' He looked up. 'It says here that you carried your platoon officer back after being wounded yourself.'

They hadn't thought it could snow that Easter Monday, as they bombed and clubbed their way forward, from crater to slag heap. He'd left a red trail behind him as he'd carried the lieutenant to the rear.

The spider was trying to decide which way he should go.

The major turned back to the service record. 'Severe jaw wound, military hospital at Bedford. Convalescent hospital. Volunteered for pilot training.' He threw the file down and rubbed his eyes. 'You've been flying with this squadron for about four months. But every one of your combat reports is vague and ambiguous. With more skill than anybody else here, you've done practically nothing to distinguish yourself.'

Hook paused as if waiting for him to say something to redeem himself.

The spider had made his decision and had crawled onto the wall map, heading north from St Quentin to Cambrai.

'Upset about Lloyd, are you?'

'Yes, sir.'

The major was doing his best for him. But there was really nothing much he could say, except that he and Lloyd had shared for all those four months. He couldn't tell him that he could never really make up his mind who the enemy was, or that his jaw was aching and he needed a drink.

Hook sighed hugely. 'I would like to see some evidence of your meeting your obligations in the future. As it stands, I am going to say in my report that you have been under stress, but this doesn't excuse your behaviour this afternoon. I will say that you have been severely reprimanded and that you regret what you did. And now, Corby, try to keep out of my sight for a few days.'

So that was that. He went out into the dark and stood for a while, looking across at the shafts of light from the open flaps of the canvas hangars. He didn't want to go over there and check his machine ready for the morning. He didn't feel hungry, and he didn't want to go to the mess and join in Smith's victory party for killing Steiner. In fact, he didn't know what he wanted to do. Mary's letter was still on his locker, but he didn't want to read it again, or answer it.

He walked slowly back to the hut. It felt lonely without Lloyd, and Harvey had gone to the party. His flask was still half full. He piled the last of the coal on the stove and sat next to it, staring at the red glow, and taking an occasional swallow from the flask. He knew what he would like to do. He would like to write a letter to Jean

Stacey. But it didn't do to write letters when you were feeling sorry for yourself. Anyway, she probably wouldn't want to hear from him. There were, after all, other men in her life. There had been the young, golden-haired second lieutenant who had openly stayed with her in the small flat across the mews. The neighbours had said it was shocking, a young woman like that sharing her flat with an officer, and it seemed altogether worse when they learned that he was her cousin.

When he'd come home on convalescent leave, after his jaw had mended, he'd understood about Jean Stacey and her cousin. It was obvious that the poor sod was a shell-shock case, and she was looking after him. In the mornings the young officer would leave her flat about half an hour after she had gone to work at the pharmacy in the hospital. He would return with her in the evening. Then they were alone together, behind the drawn curtains of the windows. Did he share her bed?

For some reason that he barely understood, he felt an affinity for the officer, but for Jean Stacey he felt a strange and slightly intoxicating combination of lust and anger.

The pair of them never seemed to go anywhere, except on one occasion. Marten had turned the corner of the mews, and there she was, alighting from a cab with the god-like young man. He'd tried to pretend he hadn't noticed them, until she called his name.

Embarrassed and angry, he'd stayed while she asked him about his wounded jaw. The young man smiled loftily, as well-intentioned officers do in the presence of lance corporals, then stammered out the question, 'Where w-were you w-wounded, Corporal?' The words were blurted hurriedly, as though he were afraid that he wouldn't manage to get through them.

'North of Arras, sir.'

'I was th-there too, near Lens. Lost nearly all my pl-platoon.'

The anger left him. 'It was bad at Lens, sir.'

The young man suddenly smiled warmly. 'That ribbon on your tunic. It's the DCM, isn't it? G-good for you.' He took a deep breath, conscious again of his rank, and added, 'Well, I wish you the best of luck, Corporal.' And to avoid the embarrassment of formal saluting, stuck his hands in his pockets.

'Good luck to you, sir.'

Jean Stacey asked him, 'When does your leave end, Marten?'

'The day after tomorrow.'

'Each time we meet it's merely to say hello and goodbye.'

He shrugged. 'It's the war.'

She smiled. 'This time I'll just say goodnight.'

The pair of them turned away. He heard them outside her front door as he went to his own. She was feeling in her bag, and he heard the young man say, 'I have my k-key here, Jean. Allow me.' And the door clicked behind them.

He'd seen Mary the next evening. Looking back now, it must have been around then that he'd started to make those unfortunate comparisons. And now Mary's human frailty was revealed through her attempts to manipulate Peter. Peter could have her, providing he stayed in England.

Who could blame her? She was a casualty of the war, just as he was. After all, he hadn't anticipated his own steady groping for the whisky bottle.

The stove had burned low and he was cold. He would have one more drink, then he'd go to bed. Tomorrow he would have to go through Lloyd's things and get Bates to send them off. It hadn't been a very good day.

Seven

IT HAD COME as a bit of a shock to learn that Lloyd was still alive. Roper sent the message to him and Harvey, late in the morning as they sat going through Lloyd's things. They had already passed onto Donovan the collection of French postcards that Lloyd had inherited from Garfield, long since buried. Marten was vetting the contents of Lloyd's writing case, while Harvey checked the pockets of the uniforms before giving them to Bates to pack, because there are, after all, things that parents need not know about their sons. It was a job that he and Lloyd had done together in the past, for other, briefer occupants of the hut.

In the writing case there was a letter from Lloyd's father, and an unpaid tailor's bill. There was also a letter from a girl named Diane. She regretted that she must break off her unofficial engagement to Lloyd. She had fallen in love with Tom. They were to be married the following week because Tom had been transferred to another Ministry job in London. She and Tom felt dreadful about all this. The letter was dated the third of November, 1917. That was about the time Lloyd had been depressed, talking of the replacements.

Marten sat and pondered for a moment, then carefully put the letter back. At that moment the orderly brought the note from Roper.

'Good God! Harvey, listen to this. "*Lloyd critically injured. In Military Hospital, Hazebrouk.*"' It gave him a bit of a lift. But immediately he began to feel uneasy, because he knew he'd have to go and visit Lloyd, and there was no denying that close contact with the wounded always nauseated him.

He left Harvey and Bates to finish off the packing of Lloyd's things and went in search of Drinkwater.

Benge called to him as he passed between the huts. 'I hear old Lloyd is still alive.' He grinned. 'The sod has probably been in The Lantern all this time with bosomy Michelle.'

He found Drinkwater in his hut, writing a letter. Smith was leaning back in a chair with his feet on top of the stove.

'Hello, Corby, what can I do for you?' Drink didn't stop writing so it was clear that he wouldn't welcome a protracted visit.

'Lloyd is in hospital at Hazebrouk. He's in bad shape. I'd like to visit him. Do you think you could juggle the roster and move my day off forwards?'

Drink stopped writing and looked at the list pinned to the wall over his bed. 'Yes, I'll switch you with Donovan. That means you can go tomorrow. Tell Donovan, will you?'

Donovan wasn't in his hut, and as it was nearly lunchtime he went over to the mess. Roper introduced him to one of the new replacements and they sat together at the long table, but within minutes he'd forgotten the man's name. Was his memory finally going? Or was it because he really didn't want to remember? He'd kept forgetting to answer Mary's letter. If he wrote to her he would have to explain to her why Peter hadn't been able to go along with her plans.

Peter was due back at the end of the week. Then Smith would be going on leave and he'd be collecting his Military Cross at Buckingham Palace! And they talked about *his* luck! Smith should back the horses. But Smith didn't seem very happy about going. There was that difficulty with his wife, going off with his younger brother like that. Maybe Smith preferred to be here, with problems he knew how to contend with.

Donovan came in and they settled the business of the day off. Then Carver was looking at his watch because he was leading the patrol. It was time to go.

Carver took them over the north side of the ridge. The Guards of the XIV Corps were down there, straddling the railway line running north-east to Staden. And there were thousands of bloody Huns just back from the Russian front, so it was said, because the Russians had all but packed the war in. They weren't daft, were they?

Marten had just begun to think that they'd get through the patrol without incident when he saw the Pfalz scouts flying on a parallel course. He fired a few rounds to attract Drink's attention and pointed.

The Huns must have seen them but they weren't running. Decoys! He craned his head back, searching the sky again as he followed the others, steering to intercept.

He knew, with absolutely certainty, that there were other Huns up there, waiting. And as the Pfalz scouts broke formation, splaying outwards, he caught a sudden flicker of reflected light above and to the left. Sleek Albatrosses, flying very high, were dropping down on them, and suddenly the sky was crowded with wheeling, skidding machines.

The wind was carrying them too far over the enemy side. They'd have to turn back. A Pfalz crossed his path with an SE chasing it. If he turned he could get an oblique shot at it. But the Pfalz had a yellow tail fin so he skidded round and fired at a dull red machine. The sky was criss-crossed with tracer trails. His jaw was set, rock hard, and his lungs full of the fumes of spent cordite. Then he saw the flare. Carver was signalling to them to break off and they clustered in on him as the Huns turned east. The Pfalz with the yellow tail fin raked an SE then climbed fast with Smith chasing it. The stricken SE turned sluggishly to the west, a thin blue vapour streaming out from behind the cockpit. God Almighty! It was Benge.

They all grouped themselves round Benge, as though it were possible to help him. Benge was trying to lose height without fanning the vapour into a flame. It didn't matter any more which side of the front he landed, as long as he could get down before the plane caught fire. They could see Benge quite clearly, rubbing his face with the sleeve of his coat as the blue vapour turned to a gushing, dirty brown torrent, and a bright yellow flame licked back along the fuselage. Benge was beating at the flames with his hands, then in despair he covered his face with his arms. The blazing machine rolled slowly onto its back. Then it exploded leaving only a dirty trail of smoke hanging in the air, and bits, small bits, fluttering down.

He felt sick. Yes, he would like to vomit, if that was all right with everybody. The setting sun coloured the clouds a fierce, angry red along the horizon, as though God and His angels were outraged by mankind.

He still felt sick that night, when he went to bed. He'd known for a long time that his position was becoming increasingly untenable. Not firing on that yellow-tailed Pfalz, and Bengy going down a few minutes later! He'd got to make up his mind where he stood.

Harvey was groping in the darkness. A match flared and he lit a cigarette. 'Corby, you awake?'

'No.'

'Did you feel worried about the LVG? The one you shot down. And those two guys stuck in it?'

Harvey probably had Benge on his mind as well. Or just the fear of burning.

'Yes. I only did it to spite Smith, so it was a particularly dirty thing to do.'

'You did what you're paid to do.'

'Yes, but I did it for the wrong reasons. And today I let one go.' It was that other skirmish with Yellow Tail, four months ago, that had started all of this. 'In that fraction of a moment as it crossed my sights, I hesitated because I didn't really want to shoot at it.'

Harvey pondered in the darkness. The red end of his cigarette made a sweeping movement. 'Jesus! What a complicated life you lead.'

'I'll grant I'm peculiar, but not unique.' Yellow Tail could easily have killed him that other time, but had chosen not to. So Yellow Tail wasn't a killing machine, but a man with the same uncertainties as himself.

Harvey sat up. 'Smith says, "If you can't ride two horses at once you shouldn't join the circus".'

'The Killer has no talent for introspection.'

'Tell me, Corby, I've got to know. Do you go through this nightmare of self-questioning every time you go to the latrine?' Harvey fell back on his bed again. 'You really are a very odd guy. Imagine having talent and not being able to use it. If I could handle an SE like you, I'd take on the Red Baron himself.'

Harvey probably would at that. With only a few weeks in the war, he was quite sure of himself, plagued by no misgivings. It must be good to be sure of yourself, to hold opinions and values firmly.

He thought Jean Stacey was probably like that. You couldn't deny that a young woman who took a man to live in her flat, even though he was her shell-shocked cousin, had clearly demonstrated a determination to go her own way without too much self-doubt. Weeks had elapsed after he'd met her in the company of the young, stammering officer, and although he had managed to get home from the flying school at Hounslow for an afternoon almost every week, he'd only seen her on one occasion. It was indelibly marked in his memory as the day he had actually touched her.

His mother had wanted a photograph of him in his Flying Corps cadet uniform. And he wanted to please her, because God only knew what the future had in store. So he'd gone to the photographer near the Metropolitan Music Hall in Edgware Road. Then the air raid siren sounded, and the photographer dropped the photographic plate and scuttled down to the basement, leaving him sitting there in front of the camera feeling like an idiot.

He could hear the far-off thump of bombs above the traffic noises, and policemen blowing their whistles to get people off the streets. He left the shop and walked towards Praed Street. Crowds were gathering, despite the policeman's whistles, and they were looking up at the tiny specks in the sky, a long way over to the east, and the white puffs of anti-aircraft shells bursting ineffectually.

Two of the specks strayed to the west, coming much closer in a wide arc that would carry them over Hyde Park. They were big Gothas. Some of the anti-aircraft guns were tracking them and it was bloody madness to stand out of cover because the shell splinters would come rattling down any minute. He'd shouted that they'd better get off the street, but of course, being civilians, they didn't understand and stayed there gawping. Then he saw Jean Stacey in the crowd, on the corner of Praed Street.

He pushed his way through to her and seized her arm. Startled, she looked at him and smiled.

'Marten! Where have you come from?'

'Quick! Get under cover.' He pushed her back against a door sheltered by a narrow alcove.

'What on earth are you doing? There are no bombs falling now.' Her head was tilted back and her wide-set eyes looked questioningly up at his face.

The shells were bursting almost overhead, and already he could hear the splinters whistling down. He leaned

116

against her, pushing her hard back against the door. Now she looked shocked but amused.

'Marten, I would be grateful if you would let me breathe a little.'

The splinters cracked down onto the roofs and into the street. There was a tinkling of broken glass and a woman screamed. The crowd panicked and began scrambling for cover. The doorway was too shallow. Marten stretched up his arms and held the lintel for support as people pushed against him, trying to squeeze into the narrow space.

He looked down at Jean. 'Don't move. Just stay as you are until the splinters stop falling.'

She stayed quite still, her eyes on his face, and her breasts pressed hard against his tunic. How firm her mouth was. It curved very slightly downwards at the corners, yet her lips were full.

The Gothas were turning away towards the east, and the shell bursts followed them. He had a brief, warm, sad feeling, because the moment had passed, and he stood back from her. She stayed in the doorway for a moment, looking up at him.

'Thank you, Marten.' She smiled.

Somebody was calling. 'There's a man hurt here.'

'Shall we see if we can help?' She paused for a moment longer, as if waiting for some indication from him.

He nodded and stood aside.

A man was nursing his gashed right forearm against his shirt. 'I dunno which is worse, the bloody Huns or our own guns!' He held up a jagged shell splinter with his left hand.

'I work at the hospital. I think I ought to get you there quickly,' Jean said. Nobody seemed surprised that she should take charge of the wounded man.

Marten stopped a passing car, but it was small, and there was only room alongside the driver for Jean and the casualty. Jean turned as she was about to get into the car. 'Hello, and goodbye again.'

He shrugged. 'We must stop meeting this way. People will begin to talk.'

She smiled, and then she was gone.

He hadn't had the photograph taken. It had become one of his many superstitions.

Lloyd had tried to get him to go into St Pol so that they could have their picture taken together, but he wouldn't. And now he wished he had, because you didn't find many friends like Lloyd.

Harvey had fallen asleep. He could hear him breathing softly. He lay awake for a while longer, wondering about tomorrow, and Lloyd, and the hospital.

The next morning he left immediately after breakfast. A sergeant and an air mechanic were taking a Crossley tender out to the wreck of Lloyd's plane to see if any parts could be salvaged, so he'd arranged to ride with them as far as the Nieppe Forest.

He sat next to the sergeant, who drove with studied carelessness born of long experience of the road, barely slowing to pass the plodding farm carts. The rain drizzled down without pause, splashing in under the canvas flap and soaking the sleeve of his greatcoat.

They passed a mound with a marker indicating unidentifiable dead; probably bits of bodies they'd found after a small gain. 'Known unto God.' Like the sergeant who'd thrown himself on the grenade. He'd been a pig of a man. But in that moment as his body was torn apart, he'd posed a nagging question.

The rain splashed across the windscreen of the Crossley. On the edge of the forest they passed soldiers, resting, sitting on the wet ground under the dripping trees.

Their uniforms were mud-stained from the trenches. They stared at the tender as it passed, wearily indifferent.

Marten could remember sitting like that, soaked through and exhausted. And it was the feeling of hopeless resignation that invariably inspired some weary wit to repartee.

'Send it down, David, send it down. My boots aren't full yet.'

'Dear Mother, the army's a bugger; sell the pig and buy me out.'

'Dear John, pig's gone, soldier on.'

'Are we downhearted?'

'You bet your bloody life we are.'

So when you looked back at it, somehow it didn't seem quite so bad after all. What was it the old man had said to Jean Stacey that time? Something about the good and the bad being so entwined.

The sergeant turned off the road and the Crossley bumped along a track through the forest.

'How far?'

'About two kilometres, sir. And the wreck of Mr Lloyd's machine is a little way off this track.'

They came upon a wooden marker stuck in the ground and the sergeant stopped the Crossley. They climbed out. The air mechanic blew on his hands to try to warm them. The sergeant frowned at the trees, and dragged out a box of tools.

'Not a very good place to crash, sir.'

Why did he feel so nervous? It was, after all, only a wrecked aeroplane that he'd come to see. Water dripped off the newly-bare branches.

'Right,' he said. 'Let's go and have a look.' He stuck his hands deep into his greatcoat pockets and they moved off among the sodden trees. Only the sergeant seemed indifferent to the weather.

119

Fifty yards off the track he saw a severed chocolate-coloured wing, caught high up in the branches. Wet, ripped canvas hung from it, exposing white spars. Thirty yards beyond, among the broken limbs of a pine tree, the tail and fuselage hung upside down.

A lance corporal sapper, wet cape draped around him, sat on a fallen tree trunk, his cigarette cupped in his hand to keep it dry. He watched them approaching then stood up slowly, nipped out his cigarette and put it in his pocket.

Marten knew now why he felt nervous. It was the same feeling you had when you went to a funeral. You forced yourself to look at the coffin and told yourself that it was all perfectly natural, but you didn't believe it. The lance corporal saluted him casually, then stood back as he walked over and looked up at the wrecked fuselage.

God Almighty! How could anybody survive a crash like that? He stood underneath, staring up into the cockpit. The engine and main fuel tank had been thrust backwards, pushing the instrument panel off its mountings. The panel had been sawn through, no doubt to get Lloyd out. The earth below the machine was black and slippery where the oil had drained.

'Looks nasty, sir.' The sergeant had joined him. 'I don't think we're going to salvage much from that. The engine's a write-off and all those instruments are busted; compass, ASI, tachometer, oil pressure gauge, the lot.'

'Got blood all over them,' the sapper said.

So they settled for the Lewis gun. The sergeant took a hacksaw from his tool box and they held the bent gun mounting while he sawed through it.

They looked around finally at all the wreckage scattered among the dripping trees.

'Well, that's about all we can do, sir.'

'Yes. We might as well go.'

They gave the sapper a lift to the main road and dropped him off. The sergeant thought for a moment. 'We're not expected back for a while, sir. Would you like us to take you onto Hazebrouk? We'd like to know how Mr Lloyd's getting on.'

'Thanks,' he said. He was glad to have company, and the comparative warmth of the Crossley cab.

So they went on together, and the sergeant talked most of the way, which was soothing somehow because that wreck had upset him a bit. The sergeant reminded him a little of the sepia photograph of the old man, on the wall of the parlour back home. Sergeants had a sort of corporate, timeless likeness.

'Nearly there now, sir.'

Hazebrouk had the forlorn appearance of all the towns close to the fighting area, worsened now by the steadily-falling rain. There were gaps in the houses of the main street, and shorn-up buildings, relics of the bombing back in September. It took nearly twenty minutes to find the hospital, situated on the northern end of the town close to the railway line. White-swathed wounded, with capes draped over them to protect them from the rain, were being carried out of the dark, grim building and loaded uniformly into the backs of waiting ambulances.

'They're taking them to the hospital train, sir. It picks up wounded from Merville, then more here, and then more from the hospital at St Omer.'

Marten nodded. He took the flask from his pocket and had a couple of swallows from it.

'You two have a drink while I'm gone.' He handed the sergeant the flask. 'It'll keep out the cold.'

'We'll save you one, sir.' The sergeant looked at him steadily.

He was scared of what he would see in that building, and the sergeant knew it. He climbed down from the tender and walked between the ambulances to the door of the hospital.

The strong, sweet smell of decay mingled with the smells of iodine and disinfectant. It was enough to make you retch. How those orderlies could do that job all day, he didn't know. Maybe it was better than being at the front. A middle-aged nursing sister with South African campaign medal ribbons on her cape directed him to the officers' ward. He paused at the doorway, not wanting to go in.

The thing was to detach oneself from it all; think of oneself as somebody else, and walk between the lines of closely-packed beds.

Then he saw Lloyd.

But it didn't look like Lloyd at all. He was lying flat on his back, his eyes closed, and his face was sunk in somehow. His hand moved slightly.

He took the hand and squeezed it gently.

'Hello, Lloyd.'

The eyes opened and focused slowly. Then a faint smile flickered across the mouth. 'Corby!' His voice was very weak. 'Good of you to come.'

He shrugged. 'I was passing. I thought I'd just look in and pick up that two pounds you owe me.'

Lloyd nodded and smiled again.

A VAD with a red stripe on her sleeve came over to him. She looked tired and irritated.

'You should have waited at the door,' she said.

'I'm sorry.'

She looked at Lloyd and her face relaxed as she moved his pillow slightly. 'How nice for you to have a visitor, Lieutenant. But he mustn't stay for long because you are rather tired, aren't you.'

It wasn't really a question, and Lloyd didn't respond.

'No. I'll only stay a minute,' Marten said. He meant it

because it depressed him, seeing old Lloyd like that. So he'd just say a few things to jolly the poor chap along, then he'd leave.

But she went and fetched him a chair which, duty driven, he had to squeeze between the beds and sit on. Now he was trapped in that narrow space.

'You had me worried,' he said. 'Bengy reckoned you were dossed down with Michelle somewhere, but you look as if you've been upstairs with Madame.'

Little jokes weren't going to work because Lloyd didn't have the strength to rise to them. He whispered, 'How is Bengy?'

'Oh! Oh, he isn't bad. Same as always. Sends his regards. They all send their regards.'

Lloyd frowned and muttered, 'He's dead, isn't he? I had a dream. Bengy's plane was on fire.'

'Yes. But it was quick. The plane blew up.'

'Good.' Lloyd closed his eyes again. There was no drive left in him. He was just lying there, waiting for it to happen.

'Lloyd. You'll be going home soon. You have to count your blessings, don't you? There's another big push about to begin. The squadron is being moved south. You'll miss it. You're lucky to be out of it.'

The eyes opened, staring up at the ceiling. Lloyd licked his lips and said softly, 'I think my luck has all run out. I needed some of yours.'

'Not true, Lloyd!' And for God's sake, his voice was beginning to sound urgent, because he couldn't just sit there and agree with Lloyd that he was done for. 'You'll go home. And you'll have a nice long rest. But you have to get a grip. Do you hear?'

Lloyd nodded his head slightly, but he didn't believe it. And if he didn't believe it he'd never get as far as Calais.

The voice was very faint now, and he had to put his

head down close to Lloyd's.

'I didn't hear you, Lloyd. Say it a bit louder.'

Lloyd whispered, 'This is not like you, Corby.' The smile creased his face again. 'You were always doom-ridden. And you've got a rule, not to get too involved in other people's affairs. Can't you leave a fellow alone to die in peace?'

And God! That came as a nasty shock! To actually hear Lloyd say it. The visit wasn't working out the way he'd intended.

The ward sister was at the foot of the bed, indicating with her eyes that he should go now. But he couldn't leave, not with old Lloyd this way.

'Lloyd! Listen to me. Dying isn't just a matter of the body packing up. You can hold on. You can make it back to England.'

The ward sister was going to get insistent. She had moved to the back of his chair. 'I think you had better go now,' she said firmly.

Lloyd's lips moved, so he tilted his head right down to hear him. 'Thanks for coming, Corby.' He gave a little sigh. 'I'm so bloody tired.'

A nurse had come over to join the sister. And the sister had her hand on his shoulder. 'I think you're upsetting him. You must leave now. He needs to rest.'

Marten pulled his shoulder away from her. 'No, he doesn't need to bloody rest!' He turned back to Lloyd. 'If you give up now, Lloyd, you're done for.'

'Please!' The sister was tugging at his arm.

'Lloyd! Do you hear me? You're not a fellow to just give up and die. You've got more guts than that.' He grabbed Lloyd's hand.

'If you don't leave now, I'll have you forcibly removed.' The sister turned to the nurse. 'Get the orderlies, quickly.'

Lloyd's eyelids flickered, then opened, and he looked up, puzzled.

Marten squeezed the limp hand. 'I'm counting on you to get back home, Lloyd.' He got up and faced the sister. 'All right. I'll go now.'

He walked quickly out of the ward, then along the corridor. He didn't really notice where he was going until he was outside again in the pouring rain. When he got back into the Crossley the sergeant handed him the flask. He swallowed down what was left of the whisky.

'Mr Lloyd bad, sir?'

'Yes. He's bad.'

'Pity.' The sergeant started the engine and banged it into gear. 'Mr Lloyd was a good man.'

He was shocked, that's what he was. Shocked to find Lloyd like that, though God knows, he'd been told the poor fellow was in a bad way, and he'd known it. All the way to the hospital he'd known it. But he was also shocked at himself for talking to Lloyd like that. It was all very disturbing, because his plan to keep himself detached and mouth a few jokes and some gossip had fallen instantly to pieces. He hadn't been able to do it.

Wasn't it always the way? You made a rule not to get too involved, because life was complicated enough. Then people went and upset it. He really had been quite out of character, ranting at Lloyd. After all, if Lloyd wanted to give up, who was he to say he shouldn't? There was no denying he had behaved ridiculously. Though perhaps it was characteristic of him to start getting involved when it was all too late. Poor old Lloyd probably wouldn't last through the night.

And now that he stopped to think about it, he'd always taken Lloyd for granted and never given him much support. Why hadn't Lloyd been able to tell him about the girl, Diane, who'd broken off the engagement for that fellow, Tom? He knew the answer. It was just as Lloyd had said. He'd made that rule.

He was depressed all the way to St Eduarde. The bloody rain went on and on. Pour it down, David, pour it down. My boots aren't full yet.

The air mechanic had huddled down and gone to sleep, and the sergeant didn't say much. They reached the airfield early in the afternoon, and he knew as soon as they passed the guard that something was up. Men were milling about everywhere, and things being loaded into lorries. So the move south was on.

Eight

HIS COUGH was definitely getting worse. Marten gasped. That was what a couple of weeks in a wet tent did for you. They hadn't expected the move south to be all beer and skittles, but for God's sake! Tents in November! And they were crawling with huge, obscene insects. They must have struck just the right combination of dim light and fetid dampness to promote their growth. Only Lewis had really believed that the move south was to give them a rest. But these days Lewis tended to believe anything that gave him hope.

The Camel pilots had the other end of the field, all snug in Nissen huts. So it was all right for Camel pilots. He could hear them running up their engines. They were to be the first planes used in the new big push.

Harvey began to shave. 'What's the weather like?'

Marten poked his head out of the canvas flap, and the cold air started his cough off again.

'Bloody dreadful,' he called. 'Typical attack weather.' He looked across the dark field as the first of the Camels, a grey shape in the gloom of the winter morning, snarled towards the tents then lifted sluggishly with its extra load of twenty-pound bombs. One by one the others followed, disappearing into the low, thick mist.

Marten began to shave hurriedly but carefully, because if he was shot down he wanted to look decent. At least he'd got some new boots, though old Roper, landed with more paper work while the equipment officer was in hospital, having his duodenum or whatever probed, had got a bit testy about them. Maybe his piles were giving him trouble. But it had been a bit unreasonable. He'd been flying with a great hole in his left boot ever since he'd crashed at Poelkapelle, and the hole had got bigger. The bloody cold had got through that hole and frozen his leg. Anyway, and this was the real crux of the matter, he'd got this sudden obsession about dying in a respectable pair of boots. He'd said so to Roper, then got slightly nasty when Roper reminded him that he'd left the revolver and the time-piece in the wrecked plane back at Poelkapelle. What the hell. Perhaps Roper would like to get up off his piles and try flying again? And Roper gave him the chit for the boots.

Everybody was short-tempered. Even Peter, with his major's crowns, and carrying the load now that Hook had gone to a job at Group, had lost his usual composure. They were all saying that he'd changed since he got back from leave. But after all, the poor chap had the whole squadron to worry about now, and maybe trouble with Mary too.

Marten swabbed his face. 'Stick close today,' he said to Harvey. 'Drink has paired us. Don't do anything daft.' And as he spoke the preliminary bombardment started.

He looked at his watch. Six-twenty. Dead on time of course. He went over to the hangars to check with Duncan.

'The revs are a bit down, sir. It's probably the weather. But I don't think you'll have any trouble today.'

That was a joke. Marten handed Duncan a cigarette and lit one himself, and it started off his cough again. His hands were steady but his stomach was in a knot, and his jaw had started to tingle preluding pain.

'You've got a nasty cough there, sir.'

'Bloody tents. Pneumonia is inevitable.'

There was a slight lull in the thump of the guns, then they began again. That meant the barrage had shifted and the tanks and infantry were moving forward. He'd better eat something, though the thought of food made him feel slightly sick. He went over to the mess tent. In just under an hour A and C Flights would be on their way over the front, and by then the Huns would probably have every available machine up there waiting for them. And by tomorrow, when Ludendorff was sure that the attack on Cambrai wasn't just a diversion, he'd be calling in squadrons from other parts of the front.

Everybody was in to breakfast. Donovan seemed in good spirits, waving a silk stocking. 'She gave it to me last night. I'm going to wear it round my neck to keep the cold out.'

Peter had gone up early to test the weather, and he came back with the news that the cloud base was down to eighty feet. Marvellous!

The conversations hung for a moment as the Camels roared back, low over the tents, to load, reload and bomb up once more. Harvey paused, listening and counting. 'They haven't all got back.' He went back to hastily scribbling a letter.

'Are you writing to your grandpa to offer him our tent? He might need it if he goes gold prospecting again.'

'Hell no! Even the Indians don't want it. I'm writing to my dad to tell him to sell the pig and buy me out.'

Peter appeared. 'Fifteen minutes, gentlemen.'

Then it was seven-ten. Peter was there to see them off, along with Zac, and Carver because his machines wouldn't be needed until mid-morning. Even old Roper came out to watch, huddled down in his greatcoat and standing back out of the blast of the propeller as Stansfield's machine swung round to face the field. And A Flight took off, the planes engulfed in mist within seconds of leaving the ground.

Anxiety was getting to Marten and it was an effort to look composed as Harvey walked over, tense but smiling. He threw down his cigarette and carefully crushed it under the heel of his boot. 'Take care, and stick close.'

'You take care yourself,' Harvey said.

Drink was getting into his cockpit. It was seven-twenty.

Things didn't go at all the way they'd expected. Drink led them low over Havrincourt Wood, then north-east flying just below the cloud base. The 37th Brigade was below them; East Surreys, Buffs, and the West Kents, all moving forward in groups behind the tanks. Marten had never seen so many of the huge, clumsy monsters. Blue smoke belched out behind them as they lurched on, crunching the barbed wire and dragging it along behind them like washing on a line as they snorted and heaved over the Hun forward trenches.

Then the tanks were behind them as they flew through the smoke screen laid ahead of the advance. The ground began to rise and Marten had to ease up the nose of the machine to clear the shattered trees and fretted walls of collapsed buildings.

Flesquires was almost completely hidden under a thick pall of dust and smoke, mushrooming up towards the cloud base. Nobody had anticipated that they wouldn't be able to see a bloody thing to shoot at down there. They flew around in circles, looking for a way down through the smoke, losing sight of each other in the thickening, menacing swirls. And that was where things started to go wrong.

Marten hauled up out of the smoke and noticed that Harvey was missing. So he flew alongside Drink and rocked his wings. But Drink was already leading them towards Bourlon Wood and merely glanced uncompre-hendingly in his direction. Drink had said that if any of them got lost they should look for him in the area of Bourlon Wood and Fontaine. But Drink had paired him with Harvey, so it would do no harm to drop back and have a quick look because he could always find Drink again later.

He turned back and approached the smoking hump of Flesquires again. But there was no sign of Harvey. He returned towards Bourlon again, still flying very low. Now no sign of Drink or the others. And the weather was appalling. No wonder he'd seen no Huns. The cloud was down to sixty feet and gusty squalls were rocking the machine. He kept going all the way to Cambrai then turned again, flying in a figure-of-eight pattern, waiting for Drink to turn up. Whenever the ground cleared below him he machine-gunned anything that moved.

But there was no point in staying. His guns had to be nearly empty. The others must have gone home. So he turned westwards. Graincourt was below and he could see the flashes from guns just south of the village. He emptied his guns into them. The British tanks couldn't have got that far yet. Then he steered two-one-zero, flying over the battle until he could see Havrincourt once more. Water splashed up from his wheels as he touched down on the sodden airfield. He'd only been gone an hour yet it felt like a lifetime.

Duncan climbed up onto the starboard foothold as he rolled to a stop. 'Are you all right, sir?'

He sat quite still for a moment then pulled up his goggles and eased himself out of the cockpit. 'Where are the others?'

'They're not back yet, sir. You're the first.'

Then came the first stab of guilt. He rubbed the clammy sweat from around his eyes. Two riggers were standing, curious and concerned, at a respectful distance.

'It was a bad one then, sir?'

'Couldn't see much for the smoke.'

Duncan was examining the fuselage. 'Only two holes, sir.'

Jesus! Every Hun soldier from Flesquires to Cambrai had shot at him, and he'd only got two holes!

Another machine flew low overhead, engine blipping, and touched down. It was Harvey, thank God.

The pilots of B Flight had begun to gather, sensing catastrophe. Harvey had swung his machine round and was taxiing back towards the canvas hangars, gunning his engine. A large piece of fabric trailed from under his port wing.

Captain Carver walked over, an unlit cigarette dangling from his lips. Harvey was climbing from his cockpit. His movements were jerky and his face looked old. He ripped off his helmet.

'Sorry I lost you all. It was the smoke and the low cloud.'

'It's all right. It couldn't be helped.'

'Where's Drinkwater and the others?' Carver's cold, impassive glance took in the two machines and Harvey, then rested on him.

'I lost Drink after I'd searched for Harvey. I looked for him over Bourlon Wood but I couldn't find him. The weather was so bad I thought he must have come back.' Why did he feel guilty?

Harvey couldn't keep still. He pushed his hands through his hair and rubbed his face with his scarf.

Another SE roared over and Marten could see the leader's streamers fluttering from the interplane struts. The plane made a half circuit and came in downwind, one wing low and much too fast, bouncing clumsily, lurching into the air and thumping down again. They watched as it ran up the field, slowing to a stop a hundred yards from them, the propeller milling as the engine idled.

For a moment they stood quite still, watching it, then Drinkwater's mechanics began running. And Marten began running after them, encumbered by his flying boots. What would they find when they got there?

Harvey and the others were just behind him as, sweating and coughing, he reached the machine. One thing was certain, he'd never make the Olympics.

'Captain Drinkwater is hurt, sir.' A mechanic stretched out his hand towards Drink's huddled back, then withdrew it as if he were afraid to touch him.

Marten pulled himself up on the starboard foothold and leaned over the slumped figure to cut the magnetos. But it was difficult because Drink's lolling head and shoulders were in the way. He dragged Drink back off the controls and Carver held him. God, there was blood everywhere! He couldn't undo the safety belt because it was wet and sticky under his groping fingers. But he must get Drink out quick or he'd vomit. 'Hold him back for Christ's sake!' The blood was gouting out over his hands.

The lolling, helmeted head was back on the headrest and Carver was pulling off Drinkwater's goggles. Drink's face was the colour of putty. The eyes opened briefly, surprised, then closed again. They hauled the heavy body out and slid it onto a stretcher.

'Don't just stand there. Get this machine over to the hangar and clean it up!' Carver was using his handkerchief to rub the blood from his hands. The mechanics began pushing on the struts to swing the aeroplane round.

Harvey had gone as white as chalk. He leaned against the tail section for a moment then turned and was sick.

Marten rubbed his hands on the wet grass. Other people's blood was distasteful, not to say sickening. Then he straightened up and took Harvey by the arm.

'Come on, we need a drink.'

Hutchens, the new man paired with Drinkwater, came back an hour later. He had mistaken Arras for Albert and had landed at Le Hameau, for God's sake. From Hutchens they learned how Drinkwater had inexplicably led him and Donovan due north of the wood, where they were attached by Hun Vee Strutters. Donovan's machine had exploded and Drink had signalled to Hutchens to get back over the front. That was the last Hutchens had seen of him. So that left three out of five.

Drinkwater died in the middle of the following morning, just before Smith got back from leave, and they buried him in the small churchyard at Lavilliers. Smith was stony-faced at the graveside, mourning for his friend.

It did no good to dwell on death that way. Marten stood behind Smith as the padre intoned the familiar words, and let his mind wander up in the hard, cold bright sky. Better to die up there, like Donovan.

Later he lay coughing on his bed in the damp tent, and pulled a blanket up over himself. There was still half an hour to go before dinner, and he might as well be miserable here as in the equally cold mess. Funerals did not suit him at all. And there were so many unfamiliar faces in the mess these days. Nearly all the old hands had gone. Where was all that good mixed up with the bad that the old man had spoken about that night, when they'd stood together in the mews with Jean Stacey?

It was odd the way his thoughts about Jean Stacey had changed. At seventeen he had seen her as a middle-class snob, slumming in the mews, enjoying her difference from them. Hot thoughts about her had kept him sleepless on many nights. But the day they'd sheltered from the air raid, he'd felt quite different about her. Her body had been pressed against his own, and he'd felt as if he had been momentarily offered something wondrous and mysterious that he knew he couldn't have. Afterwards the thought had filled him with a warm, unaccustomed melancholy. Even so, he had felt genuinely sad when he'd heard of the death at Messines Ridge of the god-like, stuttering cousin who he suspected had shared her bed.

That oddly innocent young man should never have gone back to France.

And when he'd met Jean Stacey again, after his elevation to temporary officer and gentleman, it was clear that she had changed.

It was useless to pretend that his being made an officer made no difference. It wasn't so much that she cared for officers, but rather that she didn't really relate to lance corporals. Of course, they would still have spoken briefly together. She would have asked him about his leave and talked about rationing, and he would have asked if she was busy at the hospital. But the conversation would not have become personal, as it did on that last occasion just before he'd returned to France to join the squadron. They'd walked together in the park, he rather self-conscious in an officer's uniform and with the bright new wings on his tunic, and she pausing from time to time to look at the flowers. An aged gardener, dragged out of retirement because of the war, had cut a rose and handed it to her. She held it carefully, and they walked on. And she talked to him about the death of her cousin.

They sat, resting on the grass, and he said just enough to prompt her, because he knew she needed to talk.

'David was a schoolboy such a short time ago. He was so proud when they commissioned him.' She smiled sadly and shook her head. 'And he was ridiculously patriotic, doing his bit for King and country. Even after he lost so many of his men in that battle.' She frowned. 'Where was it?'

'Lens.'

'Yes, Lens. After that he developed that awful stutter, and had nightmares. But he was still convinced that he should go back.'

'Yes.' He knew all about nightmares.

'What a good listener you are.' She turned on her side,

frowning down at the grass. 'Why on earth do men feel that they have to be soldiers and make wars?'

'Soldiers don't make wars, they endure them. And they are no worse than the statesmen who allow wars to begin. Or the civilians who are so fervently patriotic.'

'I'm not patriotic, so what can I say that David died for?'

Nothing. Another ridge. But he couldn't say that to her. 'Maybe we need a wider perspective. We can only see the here and now,' he said.

She closed her eyes and turned up her face to warm it in the sun. 'We have to live in the here and now, and make whatever sense of it we can. She sat up and faced him. 'Perhaps it's selfish of me to be so preoccupied with *my* loss. I'm alive and relatively safe. And common sense tells me that I'll be happy again, one day, when the war ends. Maybe the secret is to live from day to day, and avoid serious relationships until a time when there's something solid to build on.'

'That might be best,' he said.

'But one starts off with these sensible intentions only to find oneself caught up in the unforeseen. It was never my intention that David should become so dependent on me, or that I should feel so strongly for him. It just happened.'

'Yes.' He hadn't intended that he should want more of Jean Stacey than the warmth and softness of her body. It had just happened.

She smiled. 'I really should make an effort to forget my own troubles. There are others more in need of consolation.'

That she had done, if all the stories were true, of the succession of young officers, and some not so young, who called at the mews flat to take her out.

He lay and thought about it for a moment. The rain

spattered on the canvas of the tent. He really didn't care how many men, en route to the battles, she might have consoled. Except that perhaps one of them might have become important to her.

This cough would be the death of him. A drink or two wouldn't go amiss. Whisky was good for coughs. He got up and went over to the mess.

And wouldn't you know it, all leave was cancelled. He'd just got used to thinking he could get through the next couple of days, if he drank himself stupid every night. The odd thing was that he'd woken on the last couple of mornings with his hands shaking, but as soon as he got into the cockpit they steadied. He could go sick, of course, with his cough like that. It racked him every few minutes. But if you smoked half a packet of cigarettes before breakfast, what the hell could you expect?

Smith had drunk too much. Marten knew it as soon as they had finished dinner. Even though Smith had his back to him, there was a belligerent hunch to his shoulders. He knew it was only a matter of time before Smith turned his anger on him. Should he leave now, before the ugly scene arose? He thought not.

'Bloody Corby's luck still holds, then?' Smith had moved over to the bar, where he stood a few paces from him.

'I don't feel very lucky. Leave postponed till God knows when. But I suppose we can't be lucky all the time.' He turned away and slid his glass across to the orderly, intending to end the exchange.

But bloody Smith wasn't going to give up that easily.

'I'd say you *are* lucky. You break off from the flight and you come back with just two holes in your machine. Meanwhile Donovan's killed and Drink is shot to hell. Yes, I'd say you're very lucky.'

'All right, so I'm lucky,' he said, trying to keep his

voice down because the others were pretending not to listen.

'You also came back first.'

There was that twinge of guilt again. But to hell, he didn't have to explain his actions to Smith.

Smith was getting maudlin as well as nasty. His eyes were red and moist and his powerful arms hung loosely by his sides.

'If I'd been back from leave a day earlier, I would have been with Drink and maybe he wouldn't be dead now.'

'You can't tell because you weren't there.'

'No, I wasn't there. But I'm back now, and when I lead what's left of the flight tomorrow afternoon, nobody finds an excuse to break off and flit around in the clouds. I want you, Harvey and Hutchens protecting my backside while I find us some Huns.'

It was funny the way his hands had suddenly steadied again, and he felt ice cold inside. He raised his glass and swallowed slowly.

'Well, it's a big backside to protect. Do you think three of us will be enough?'

There was an uneasy silence, then somebody laughed. He swallowed down the rest of his drink and left.

He walked slowly towards the darkened hangars, his anger subsiding. Gusts of wind were tugging at guy ropes, and he could hear canvas flapping somewhere. Rain water had settled in small pools among the cinders. The clay soil was so thick the field would probably stay soaked all winter. Most of the planes were out in the open, lashed down against the wind, but his machine was in the large canvas hangar, out of the weather.

He flicked on the switch at the hangar entrance. The bare bulbs, lashed up under the canvas roof, glowed dimly. How the hell did the mechanics work in this light?

He stood for a moment, looking at the blunt, squared-off nose and the exhaust-streaked fuselage of his SE5. There really wasn't anything for him to do. He felt with his finger the tension on the incidence bracing wires, then looked for the two small new patches covering the bullet holes he'd picked up the day Drink had been mortally wounded. There had been other relatively quiet days when he'd come back with many more holes than that.

He climbed up into the cockpit and sat motionless, thinking about Drinkwater. Maybe Smith was right and he should have stuck with Drink. But Drink had, after all, paired him with Harvey. And he knew that his loyalty to Drink had never extended very far. If he had stayed with Drink he would have done his best for him. But it hadn't worked out that way.

Sometimes you ended up able to help somebody and sometimes you didn't. And sometimes you pushed your luck a bit harder and went out of your way to help somebody, the way he'd done, looking for Harvey. There were no real rules, and weather and circumstance could make nonsense of the orders. He might feel occasional twinges of guilt about Drinkwater, but these would diminish. There really wasn't time to feel guilty.

He'd flown around in all that shitty weather for longer than common sense decreed, hadn't he? He'd be out there again tomorrow, wouldn't he? And he really didn't expect anybody to stay and die with him if the odds got too long. If they thought he was monopolising all the luck, well then, they could register a complaint with the Luck Department. And if they didn't care to accept the limits of his loyalty, they could take him out and shoot him, and that would be all right with him too.

He rubbed his hand over his jaw. It ached a little. But he wouldn't have another drink tonight because he didn't need one. And he thought he'd sleep quite well, because coming to terms with oneself, even temporarily, relaxes a man. The problems would still be there for him to pick up in the morning, but he'd throw out some of the guilt to make the load more manageable.

He remembered what Jean Stacey had said about living from day to day. Would she be asleep now, her warm, soft body still beneath the covers? He was too tired to feel even a flickering of lust. But it would be good to talk to her. Perhaps he would write her a letter. The passing thought hardened into a certainty. Yes, he would write to her tomorrow.

He went to bed and slept soundly. And he didn't wake up until Bates shook him in the morning.

The relaxed feeling he'd had seemed to have spilled over into the new day, though his cough still racked him. Peter sent for him immediately after breakfast.

'Things haven't worked out very well, have they?' And Peter was looking worried, the way Hook always seemed to look. 'I have to say this, Marten. You shouldn't have broken off from the flight. Now I've just made Smith up to flight commander and his first request was that I should move you elsewhere.'

'Fine. Move me where you like. If you or Smith want to blame me for what happened to Drink, then I suppose that's what you must do. But the facts remain. Drink paired me with Harvey so I felt it was my responsibility to look for him, and then Drink wasn't where he said he'd be. He was miles north of Bourlon Wood when he was attacked. I'm not responsible for his death.'

Peter looked weary. 'I didn't say you were responsible for Drinkwater's death.'

'No, but the thought probably crossed your mind.'

'Dammit, don't tell me what goes on inside my mind.' Now Peter was looking annoyed. 'I've told Smith that you stay in his flight, at least until your leave. That shouldn't be long – perhaps only a matter of a few days before Wing rescinds the order and we open the leave roster again. And I'm telling you that until you go on leave you give Smith your support, regardless of how you feel about him.'

'Right.' Marten nodded slowly, frowning down at Peter's cluttered desk. 'I'll do that.'

'That's settled then.' Peter went on, 'This afternoon you're on patrol with Smith, but this morning, at ten-thirty, I want you and Harvey to escort an Ak W reconnaissance. You'll lead, of course, and I want you to take Sullivan with you because he needs experience.'

'Oh! Right,' he said, a bit surprised, because he wasn't often asked to lead anything. Was this Peter's way of saying he still had some faith in him? Or was he just hard-up for experienced pilots? He had to ask the question. 'Tell me. If Smith is so anxious to get rid of me, why are you keeping me in his flight?'

Peter smiled thinly. 'I'm not too sure that Stansfield or Carver want you either. But you might like to know that Harvey came to see me. And he asked if, in any future rearrangements I might make, he could continue to be paired with you.'

He felt warm inside, almost happy, which was odd because almost everything was going disastrously. Harvey knew what was going on.

Marten got Harvey and Sullivan sorted out.

'You stay close. And Sullivan, if we're attacked, you steer two-seven-zero and get back over the front as fast as you can. Don't wait for Harvey or me. Understand?'

Sullivan nodded and looked up at the sky. 'It's a nice day,' he said.

It was time to go, but Marten wanted to thank Harvey for what he'd said to Peter.

'Hey, Harvey.'

'Yeh?'

But he couldn't think how to say it. 'Take care.'

'You too.'

They landed briefly at Marieux then took off again, climbing slowly towards the front, with the slow, hefty reconnaissance machine a few hundred feet below and slightly ahead of them. It was the first hard, bright day they'd had since the battle began.

They flew over Flesquires and Marten could see the ruins of Havrincourt Chateau on the crest of the ridge, clear now of smoke. All the way up to Bourlon Wood had been captured by the infantry and the tanks, but the first rapid advance had slowed and it didn't look as if they'd get as far as Cambrai. There, below, was the inevitable bloody salient.

They crossed the northern rim of the battle, on the ridge at Fontaine. Shells were falling on the far side of the village. The Ak W observer was indicating north-east with his outstretched arm, so they followed the broken line of the road, skirting north around Cambrai.

Some anti-aircraft shells burst just below them, rocking Marten's machine, and it crossed his mind briefly that the SE might have suffered some damage. But there wasn't time to think about it. And nothing else untoward happened. The observer on the Ak W was waving again, and they all turned, following the Escaut towards Cambrai but heading west now.

When they were nearly back over the front Marten saw some enemy machines off to the north, and he hastily gained height, leading Harvey and Sullivan between the Huns and the reconnaissance machine. But half a dozen Camels turned up, so he left them to it and stayed above and behind the Ak W, shepherding it back until they were safely over Havrincourt.

He felt good. They'd done an honest job of work

without actually killing anybody. He could praise Sullivan when they got back. And maybe he could find some way of indicating his appreciation to Harvey. Yes, he ought to do that.

They were over Bapaume now. The Ak W pilot waved and the machine fell away to the right, heading for home. Marten waved back but kept the Ak W in sight until it was safely over its own field. Then he, Harvey and Sullivan flew due west.

The stratus clouds, orange-tinted by the sun, streaked the sky to the north. Sullivan was right. It was a nice day. Later, after the mid-afternoon patrol, he'd write the letter to Jean Stacey. What would he say to her? He might mention that he thought about her quite a lot, when he was flying back from the patrols. But he would not imply a relationship between them. Not yet. He'd perhaps tell her about the way some of the shattered trees had started to put out leaves during the summer, and how the grass was growing again, covering the old battle zone, quiet since the previous spring.

Below them was the fork in the road and the village of Laville lay just ahead. Beyond that was the airfield with the woods behind it. Harvey waved and gestured towards the bright, cold sky, his mouth curving in a wide smile.

They dropped into a steep glide, levelling out over the hangars. The possibility of battle damage to his machine crossed his mind. That shell had burst very close. But he dismissed the thought. His wheels touched the grass and he throttled back. Another one over.

There was a sharp splintering crack and the SE lurched over to starboard. Give it throttle! The engine raced, wide open. For Christ's sake lift! But he'd lost too much speed and the starboard wing was dropping. Shut off the fuel! The control stick jerked out of his hand as the wing snagged in the wet earth and ripped off. The undercarriage collapsed and the propeller splintered; and engine screaming, the nose ploughed down. His body jack-knifed and his face smashed into the front of the cockpit.

He was suspended in space, face downwards in a thick grey mist. He could smell petrol but it didn't matter because he was surely dead. Fire couldn't hurt him now. Voices a long way off called to him. Then hands were pulling on his shoulders.

The grey mist was clearing a little. Why was the compass under his face? Hands were under his arms and the voices sounded urgent. He was being dragged backwards. He'd done that for Drinkwater, but that was a long time ago, in another life. Somebody was holding his collar, preventing his face from falling forward again, and a hand was undoing his safety belt. He felt a violent pain as he tried to speak and blood splashed out of his mouth onto the instruments. And there was the helpless feeling of being lifted, carried, and lowered to the ground.

The goggles were being pulled from his head. He was on his back, swallowing blood and choking. He'd have to push up on his elbow, and cough, and spit blood.

There, that was much better. And in the greyness he could see faces all round him, curious and concerned. Harvey was kneeling, looking down at him, and he heard him say, 'Oh Christ!' But it surely wasn't so bad. He'd have to tell Harvey he was all right, but there was the pain again. His mouth wouldn't open properly and only a harsh sound came out. He choked and retched. And there was Peter kneeling next to him, and he didn't seem to mind the blood splashing onto his uniform. If he stretched out his hand and gripped Peter's arm, Peter would know that he didn't need to worry about him. But he couldn't stop coughing. And night was coming on fast, and the voices were distant now.

Nine

HE HUDDLED DOWN inside his greatcoat and stared at the rain, spattering across the window of the railway carriage. Water was running off the slate roofs of the sad, grey little houses of Southwark, crowded together up close to the railway. Nothing had changed, yet it was all quite different. It had lost its look of permanence. Even a year ago the Bovril advertisements and those ugly little houses squashed between dirty wharves and depots had seemed as timeless as St Paul's, towering up out of the grime and rain across the river. Now he was only conscious of decay. But it was no good feeling morbid on the first day. He'd got the whole of his convalescent leave to get depressed in.

The train clanked, slowing over the bridge. The river below looked grey and huge and choppy, and a squat tug boat was dragging a string of coal barges up river to Battersea, their wash rocking the small lighters and tenders moored up to rusting buoys. He could feel the train juddering as it pulled in to Charing Cross, and he was nearly home. How long had it been? Five months flying in France, and over three months in hospital.

He got to his feet to pull his bag down, and caught his reflection in the small oval mirror below the luggage rack. His greatcoat collar shadowed the left part of his face, but not enough to obscure the damage.

He turned away from the image, frowning to himself. What the hell could you expect? It was only one side of his face. There wasn't any point in feeling bitter about a little thing like that. After all, they'd managed to save nearly all his teeth. And a damaged face wasn't much when you thought about what could have happened. Bloody Corby's Luck was holding. He frowned again and whistled tunelessly to himself.

The train heaved to a stop and released steam shrouded him as he opened the carriage door. It was much noisier than he remembered and there were uniforms everywhere. He'd not seen American army officers before. They looked big and fit and well dressed. A couple of years in France would change all that. But for God's sake! Had he survived five months of flying over the Western Front just to be crushed by a platform trolley? And why did the bloody porter keep trying to take his bag? He could carry his own bag.

There were military police all along the barrier, but they glanced at his face and turned away. And there he was, out in the Strand. It felt good to have got this far, even though Trafalgar Square looked gloomy in the gathering dusk and restricted light.

A newsboy was calling out that the Germans were advancing on Petrograd to enforce the peace terms, but it was no good his worrying about the Russian front, he'd got troubles enough. So the thing to do was maintain an inscrutable calm and head for the Masons' Arms before going home. Maybe the old man would be there.

He was lucky and managed to get a cab in St Martin's Lane. But he needed time to think before going home, so he paid the cabby off in Edgware Road and began walking. The Metropolitan Music Hall was open, and the pie shop still in business, though God knows where they got the meat from. Even though it was dark, there was still enough bustle to suggest the old days, before the war. He turned off and walked through to Paddington Green. A tram clanged along Harrow Road, darkened and almost empty now the day was coming to an end. It was a comforting sight, that tram, with the overhead arm crackling blue sparks off the wet cable.

It was going to be a bit of a shock to his mother, his face like this. All he was really doing was putting off showing himself to her. She would be making a meal for him and fussing in the kitchen, wondering why he hadn't got home. A cold wind howled across the open space of Paddington Green, lifting the refuse and plastering a wet newspaper to his legs. It would be altogether better if he had a drink or two before he went to the flat.

Steam from the engines trundling into the Great Western Depot swirled up over the iron girders of Bishop's Bridge as he crossed. The air-raids made everybody black-out conscious, so you took your life in your hands, trying to cross the road, with the great dark lorries rumbling in and out of the goods yards. The bloody drivers were worse than the Huns, bawling at you out of the blackness of their cabs. Westbourne Grove looked grey in the dim light, and he could feel his spirits sagging as he walked through the dark, familiar streets. Now he'd reached the mews, and he was tired, but shining like a beacon for returning travellers, he saw a chink of light in the blacked-out window of the Masons' Arms.

He pushed his way into the noise and heat. The small pub smelled of beer and stale bodies, and the sawdust under his feet was dirty and beer-stained. He hadn't been in there very often because he'd rarely drank before he enlisted, but he knew all his father's drinking cronies over there in the corner, unshaven, collarless and dirty from their work in the coal wharves.

They stared, shocked, then Fred Kelly said, 'It's young Marten. Come on over.'

He tilted his head so that the good side was towards them. 'My dad been in yet?'

'No, but he shouldn't be long, unless he's waiting for you at home.'

'You're all supposed to stand up when an officer comes in, even if he's a bit knocked about.'

"Ow are you, Marten boy?' Huge, hump-backed Tommy Price knew all about being different from other people.

He twisted his face into a grin. 'Improving,' he said. 'Improving.' He'd better buy them all a drink, and just one double for himself. Then he'd go back to the flat.

Annie was still there, skinny but nice, pumping up the pints. He signalled to her and pointed to the half-empty glasses of the corner group, and she flashed her quick smile.

'Hello, Marten. Just got back then? Your dad said you were expected.' The beer gushed out of the spigot as she hauled expertly on the pump.

'I'm on my way home. I thought the old man might be drinking with his pals.'

'You'd have your time cut out, trying to keep pace with that lot.' She jerked her head towards the corner. Then she glanced at him appraisingly. 'Your face all right now?'

'Yes, it's fine.'

'You don't look very well.'

'I'm all right. You're still pretty.'

She was pushing a pint glass across to Tommy Price and scooping up another glass with her free hand. 'And you're still handsome.'

He turned sideways to smile. 'I'm beginning to feel better already.'

'Have a drink before you go?'

'Yes. Large whisky. You have one as well.'

He'd swallowed the drink down before she got back with the change and the quick smile.

'That was fast. You didn't use to drink like that. You all come back different.'

'It's the war, you know.'

'So they tell me.' She picked up the glass, washed it, and polished it with one quick sweep of her hand. 'You'd better go home now, your mum will be waiting.'

'Yes, Annie.'

'Look in again, won't you?' There was the smile again, warm and inviting. 'I've a fancy for handsome young officers.'

'I believe you.' You knew where you were with a girl like Annie.

After the first few uncertain moments, coming home wasn't so bad. His mother put the kettle on, chatting excitedly. Then she stopped, leaning on the small gas stove, and began to cry. She turned and held onto him as if she would stop anything ever hurting him again.

The old man held her shoulders. 'It's all right, my old love. He's home again.'

So he was determinedly cheerful which wasn't too difficult, because by God it was good to be back. He pretended to be hungry and told funny stories while he ate, until his mother was smiling again. The clock on the mantelpiece chimed, and the parlour was warm, with the illusion of security. His mother talked about the food queues, and the old man rambled over the campaigns of his youth, far off now, pushed back into time. It was altogether safer than dwelling on the present.

Of course, returning to the window over and over again wasn't going to bring Jean Stacey back to her flat. She didn't come home at all that night.

He filled the next morning shopping with his mother. On a quick count he'd found he was quite well off, what with all that back pay, and his poker winnings, sent onto him by Harvey. So he bought all the unrationed food he could find, and black market meat that the large food shops in Westbourne Grove were only too happy to sell to a wounded officer, at a price. He carried it all home, clumsy under the weight. In the afternoon he filled time by writing to Harvey.

But he was restless and kept returning to the window. The mews looked drab in the darkening afternoon. Before he'd enlisted, the lamplighter used to ride up on his bicycle and light the flickering gas lamp on the arch at the mews end. But the lamp stayed unlit now and the lamplighter was probably dead in France. Old Mrs Payne was walking slowly towards her door. She was dressed in black, mourning for her dead son, and it was as if the rain and the cold no longer touched her.

Marten leaned on the windowsill and felt the coldness of the glass against his forehead. The mews hadn't changed much. Life went on much as always, despite all the things that had happened to him. Some of the stables in the mews had been converted into workshops. The one below Jean's small flat was leased to a printer. He could hear the soft clacking of a machine, and occasionally the balding head of the typesetter passed across the grimy window.

He looked again at the window of Jean's sitting room. The curtains remained half opened, undisturbed since he had returned the previous evening. His mother had said Jean often stayed with her sister, widowed when the *Racoon* went down off the coast of Ireland. He rubbed his hand over his face and jaw, feeling the familiar scars. He hadn't written that letter to her. Somehow it had seemed inappropriate.

He turned away, frowning to himself. In the kitchen he could hear his mother singing, and that was odd because he hadn't heard her do that before. He slid his tunic on. It was shabby and it didn't fit properly now because he'd lost a lot of weight. He'd have to get the uniform altered or, better, buy a new one. Tailoring was a good line of business in wartime, always plenty of trade. But officers went back to the front and got killed, leaving the poor bloody tailor with unpaid bills. So even tailors had their problems.

He gave the buttons of his greatcoat a quick polish. A man ought to keep up appearances. Then he put on his cap and looked at himself in the mirror. God, he looked old! Thirty at least. And his face like that. But he'd survived. No mean achievement these days.

He whistled to himself and clumped down the narrow stairs, calling out to his mother that he was going for a walk. Then he continued down the last steep flight and out into the mews. The rain had ceased but the cobbles were still wet, and water trickled along the gutter. It was dark now, but of course there was still no light in Jean's window. He walked under the arch at the mews end, past the Masons' Arms, and on into Westbourne Grove.

It was really no good pretending to himself that he was just out for a walk. He wanted to see Jean and he might just as well admit it. His feet took him, inevitably, to Praed Street and the hospital, where he paused, uncertain what to do.

He was probably only a matter of yards away from her. And he was supposed to feel good, wasn't he? With the prospect of seeing her, perhaps any minute! So why did the pub over the road look so inviting? Maybe he was making a big mistake. Perhaps she was involved with somebody else by now. In all honesty, you couldn't expect a girl like that to be on her own for long, now could you?

People were coming and going. Two nurses passed him, laughing softly in the darkness, and one of them glanced back at him.

Through the glass panel in the door he could see the hall porter looking in his direction. It was pointless standing out here. He'd catch his death in this cold wind. He paused for a moment longer, knowing he couldn't just walk away, not now he'd got this far. But as soon as he pushed his way through the door he felt over-exposed, and very conscious of his damaged face.

'Can I 'elp you, sir?' The older porter was looking at him over the top of his wire-rimmed glasses.

'Is Miss Stacey on duty in the pharmacy?'

The old man ran his finger along a pencilled entry in his book.

'She's still 'ere, sir.' He pointed up at the rack. 'And see, she hasn't 'anded 'er keys in yet, so she's bound to come 'ere before she goes 'ome. I'd think she'd be down soon. But if you want me to, I'll let 'er know you're 'ere?'

'No. Thanks anyway. I'll wait.'

He went and sat on a hard, high-backed wooden seat near the back of the hall. The clock ticked heavily and dark, broad-framed portraits frowned down at him from the wall. Nurses and orderlies passed him, and visitors, ill at ease and concerned. Occasionally, the main door swung open, letting in more visitors and the chill night air. It was all a mistake. He shouldn't have come.

Suddenly there was Jean, starched-white-coated, crossing the entrance hall towards the old porter at his desk. A long girl, with a swinging decisive walk, so you knew exactly where she was going. She hadn't seen him yet so there was still time to retreat. Another few seconds and he would be irretrievably caught up.

She leaned over to look at a clipboard above the porter's desk, shifting her balance onto one foot, then raising the other one slightly and wiggling it, as if to give it a rest. It was strange. All that thinking about her while he was in France, and then in the hospital in Sussex, had led to here and now, with her just a few paces away, ordinary but bloody marvellous. The old porter was trying to tell her, nodding in his direction, but she was peering short-sightedly at the clipboard. That was odd because he'd never imagined her as short-sighted. She began putting her glasses on as she turned in his direction.

She stood quite still for a moment, looking at him, the glasses hanging in her hand. Then she slowly walked over.

'Marten!'

He was done for. Committed. Retreat was now out of the question.

'I didn't know you were coming home from the hospital. How are you?'

He turned his head sideways. 'I'm fine.'

She smiled. 'You look awful.'

'Well, it's been a bit of a day. Shopping. And all those people.'

She nodded, waiting for him to add something. Then she placed her hand on the back of her neck, resting it.

'I feel awful too. I haven't stopped all day.' She paused, knowing he'd come for a purpose.

He'd screwed his cap like a rag. There was a smear of dried blood on the cuff of her white coat, and he quickly looked away. Since Drinkwater's death the sight of blood disturbed him. He said it in a rush. 'I wondered if you would like to come to a concert with me tomorrow?'

There was an almost imperceptible delay before she replied. Then he thought he detected a note of caution in her voice. 'Yes. That would be nice. And we can have a talk. I'll be free after six.'

A smiling Medical Corps major strode across the hall and stopped when he saw Jean in conversation. She waved. 'I'll only be a moment, Frank.'

The major's quick glance in his direction seemed more

than just curious.

'Shall we say six then?' Jean said.

He nodded firmly, keeping the good side of his face towards her. 'Good. Till tomorrow.'

The smiling major was still standing, waiting for the brief conversation to end.

'I think he wants you. Don't work too hard.'

'Goodbye then.' And she smiled. 'It is good to see you.' Then she turned and walked off with the major.

It hadn't turned out quite the way he had thought it might, and as he walked out of the hospital he found himself frowning. But then nothing ever does turn out the way you expect. There had been that suggestion of uncertainty in her reply. Of course, he shouldn't be surprised. After all, only an idiot could believe that she'd been waiting all these months for a man with a smashed face to ask her to a concert. He whistled to himself. And time changes people, and their commitments and allegiances.

The next morning he faced up to how shabby he'd become. He looked like something in Sid Lovatt's junk shop. Even old Mr Solomons the rag picker wouldn't want this uniform. He could fill in some time by going to the tailor and getting himself fitted. His cap looked as if it had been kicked along the gutter. Old Lloyd would have picked that cap up with two fingers and dropped it in the waste bin. And wasn't it incredible, hearing from Lloyd again! All these months of thinking him dead, and now a letter, redirected half a dozen times. It didn't sound too bad. Lloyd had lost one leg, above the knee. But it wasn't as if the poor chap would have to sell matches or anything like that.

After he'd been to the tailor he took a walk in the park, and thought about Lloyd's offer of a job when the war ended. That filled in the time till nearly six o'clock. It

154

was stupid to keep looking at his watch and counting the minutes.

He met Jean in the entrance hall of the hospital, and felt completely off balance.

'Marten, how splendid you look!'

That was a bloody lie, he looked dreadful. It was she who looked splendid. And why had that bloody smiling major appeared again to say goodnight, just as they were stepping out into the darkened street? Almost as if he was trying to say something, just by his presence.

As they walked towards Bayswater Road and the possibility of a cab, he still had the major on his mind. Jean paused in the middle of the smalltalk people use to fill in the time between one place and another. 'Marten, do we have to walk so fast?'

Of course they didn't. They weren't in the bloody cavalry, were they? 'I'm sorry,' he said. He slowed his pace and surprised himself by taking her arm.

'I think your mind was elsewhere,' she said. And he felt a slight pressure from her hand.

The concert was perhaps a bit of a mistake. Jean was completely absorbed, and turned only occasionally to smile in his direction. But the music had an inexplicable effect on him. On one poignant cadence it welled up over him and he felt as if he were willingly drowning in the deluge of sweet sound. And when the sound poised for a moment before pouring over him once again, he had to clench his teeth to hold back his tears. It was disturbing to know that his nerves were that close to the surface, even after all these weeks in England. So when they came out he suggested that they have a meal, because that would give him the opportunity to drink and set himself to rights.

Seated alone with her in the restaurant, and with the opportunity he had wanted all that time in France, he didn't know what to say. She was a stranger to him.

Wasn't that always the way? You romanticise people and situations when you are away from them. Then reality turns out to be nothing like the dream. And the things you wanted to say seem inappropriate.

He fiddled with his glass, then to keep up his end of the conversation he told her the funny story about Benge landing upside down on the roof of the stores. Jean sat quite still, her arms folded, cradling her breasts. She smiled with her eyes because it really was quite a funny story and he'd told it often enough to be good at it. But it was stupid to squander the time he had with her. Worse, there was a growing weariness inside him. Maybe the dream would come to nothing.

She glanced discreetly at her watch then asked him some clinical questions about his damaged face.

'Your mother told me the surgeon removed a tiny fragment of metal, a relic of your earlier wound.'

'Yes. It's fine now. It doesn't hurt a bit.'

'But didn't it hurt, all those months while you were flying?'

He was puzzled how to explain. 'I was never really sure, whether I was imagining the pain, you see.'

Perhaps she did see, perhaps she didn't. How can another person understand a thing like that? So he changed the subject again and told her another funny story, about Donovan's dyspepsia, and how Donovan used to fly with a flask of whisky and a bottle of milk of magnesia. If one didn't work he'd try the other. All the time he was talking, the other part of his mind was concerned with how Jean could be so ordinary yet interest him so. Was it all imagined? He could see now that she was older than him. She had that slight set to her face that seems to come with maturity, and the surrendering of illusions, but it seemed to make her more interesting. There was, though, the feeling that she was holding herself back from him, and he wasn't sure why.

'You're doing it again, Marten.'

'What am I doing?'

'Part of your mind is elsewhere.'

She was very good at knowing things like that.

'How did you know?'

'Perhaps I'm a witch.' She smiled. 'Apothecaries were once only a step from witchcraft.'

'Then maybe you know of a cure for a mind that turns this way and that, recognises problems but can't settle for long enough to resolve them, tries again but grows weary and turns back in on itself again.'

This time the smile didn't go beyond her eyes. 'There are apothecaries who offer remedies for tired young heroes.'

'To which apothecary should I go?'

She paused, frowning, and toyed with her glass. 'For some, an apothecary has opiates that give temporary relief. Some apothecaries are charlatans, they offer sugared liquid. Some don't understand the nature of the ailment, so their remedies are useless.'

'But there are some who are different?'

'Yes.'

'And what do they offer?'

'Everything.'

Now she looked at him steadily. 'And others, while understanding so very well the nature of the sickness, have nothing to offer.'

He sat for a moment, looking at her. That was that then. He took a deep breath. She had warned him. At least she was honest.

He finished his drink. 'Should we leave now?'

She glanced down, peering short-sightedly at her watch. 'Perhaps we should. I have a very full day tomorrow.'

He signalled to the waiter to fetch the bill. It was odd. He felt numbly indifferent, but his hands had begun to shake.

'Yes. I'm sure you must be very busy,' he said. 'What with all the casualties from France, and the air raid victims.'

'It's not *so* bad for me. Worse for the nursing staff, and some of the surgeons didn't leave the hospital for nearly a fortnight when the Cambrai battles began.'

No doubt smiling bloody Frank was one such. With nothing much to do but saw off a few arms and legs.

'They could be worse off,' he said. There must have been something in his tone, because she glanced at him.

'Many of them have seen service in the hospitals in France.'

'Good for them.' She was probably having an affair with smiling bloody Frank. She'd only come to the concert with him out of politeness. The thing to do was to take her home and bid her goodnight with some dignity. But as he helped her on with her coat her shoulders were under his hands, weakening his resolve. And in the cab he could feel the warmth of her as they sat together. He wanted to hold her. That's all. Just hold her. He went on making conversation and the other part of his mind kept wondering what her remedy for tired young heroes would be.

He paid the cabby off at the corner of the mews, and they walked along the wet cobbles, dimly lit by chinks of light from the windows as they passed. She said how cold it had become. Snow in the air, he suggested.

They stopped in front of her door, and she stood with her face tilted up to him. It was perhaps just a trick of the half light, but now she looked beautiful.

'I'm sorry, Marten.'

And he knew why.

'I believe you,' he said.

'I could only offer opiates, or sugared water.'

'Have I asked for more than that?'

'No, but you need more than that. I can't offer you that part of myself that you deserve.'

To whom would she offer herself, then? Had she given everything to her dead cousin, and was there nothing left? What the hell difference did it make? But he had to ask. He kept his hands sunk deep in his greatcoat pockets because he didn't want her to see them shaking.

'Is that part of you to be saved then, for a *particular* tired hero?'

'Not for a hero. A hero would squander what I offer. Heroes demand too much and cannot give in return. They've already given themselves to the war.'

'I'm not like that. I'm not a hero. Can't you see that!' He was speaking much too loudly and could feel his movements becoming jerky and uncontrolled as he pulled his hands from his pockets. 'I *hate* the war. Honest. I haven't given myself to it. I'm just a tired bloody coward!'

'Hush!' She stretched out her hand and touched the jagged scars on his face. 'Look what they've *done* to you.' Her touch became a caress. 'But you'll go on telling jokes. And they'll send you back to France. And you'll go because you cannot really believe you deserve anything else.'

She slowly withdrew her hand and took a deep breath. 'You *are* a hero, Martin. If I let you, you'd complicate my life. And then you'd go away.'

He stood back from her. And he felt empty.

'All right! Have a nice, safe, uncomplicated life. Offer sugared water to officers on their way to the front. But don't get involved. Save that part of you for those who stay at home!'

She was angry now, speaking rapidly. 'Yes. I'll steer

clear of heroes. One stuttering, nervous wreck, begging to be returned to active service, was enough for any lifetime. I implored him not to go. I *knew* he would die!' She paused. 'But he went. For King and Country. And what good did it do?'

'Right,' he said. 'Right.' Now he could barely control himself and his hands moved in erratic gestures. 'So the poor sod went and got himself killed. And you'll have none of me because I might be selfish enough to get myself killed too. You'd better marry smiling bloody Frank. He'll stay alive for you.'

'Well, that makes more sense, doesn't it!' she said passionately. She turned to her door and put the key in the lock. Then she looked back over her shoulder and said softly, 'I did say I'm sorry, Marten. And I meant it.'

'Yes,' he said. 'And I'm sorry too.' He turned and walked quickly away in the direction of the Masons' Arms. But he had to struggle to regain his composure as he pushed his way through the swing doors and went to the bar.

'Whisky,' he said.

Annie poured and passed it to him with a quick, easy movement. 'Want to tell me about it?'

'About what?'

'Madam. Up the mews. Upset you, has she?'

Bloody women! They knew everything. They had some kind of bush telegraph.

'No,' he said. 'It's my Uncle Frank. He's just died and left me a million. I'm worried because I don't know what to do with it.'

'Well, you would be, wouldn't you? Don't drink so fast. It'll ruin your liver.'

He was well out of that abortive affair. He'd probably be sent back to France. And it wouldn't do to have problems on his mind. He got Annie to pour him another drink. No, it wouldn't have done. Jean disturbed him too much. In all honesty he'd been a bit soft about it all. In times like these a man was better off on his own.

'Just one more,' Annie said as he held the glass out to her. 'Then you go home and to bed.'

'Don't nag at me, Annie, there's a good girl. It's only sugared water.'

'No it isn't. And it doesn't cure anything.'

So there it was. He'd thought it all out quite sensibly. Jean had done him a favour. No doubt about it, he was better off this way.

But his hands were still shaking.

Ten

HE SLEPT BADLY. Sometime after midnight he woke, sweating and shaking from the nightmare of the burning cockpit, his hands groping with the safety belt. But it was wet and sticky and he couldn't undo it, and the revolver with its obliterating bullet was just out of his reach. Then he'd lain awake, staring up at the ceiling, and wishing the night would end. So he was a bit washed out when at last the light came and the early morning noises of the mews began.

When he had received the invitation from Mary, to have lunch with her and Stephen, he'd guessed about them right away, and he'd felt uneasy because, let's face it, he didn't want to get involved. When he got back to the squadron Peter would be bound to ask him if he'd seen Mary, and what was he to say? But he couldn't refuse her, because Mary had meant a lot to him for a long while.

So there he was, waiting in the restaurant just a short way from the War Office. The bloody place was packed with officers, munching and swilling before going back to their desks to fight their paper war. Though maybe he wasn't being fair. Some of them looked as if they had been wounded, and there were a number of grey heads, dug out from retirement, with campaign ribbons going back to the Afghan Wars.

He felt a stab of sadness when he saw Stephen, immaculate, with his well-tailored uniform and an MC ribbon, and Mary beside him. They had that look of being committed to each other, good or bad, right or wrong. And that meant the old days, of all of them being together, and Mary the prize, were finally and completely over.

162

Mary was flushed with the cold but it just made her look more attractive. She saw him before Stephen did, and he caught her shocked expression.

'Marten!' There was a faint suggestion of huskiness in her laugh which meant she was getting emotional.

It was even good to see Stephen, hardly changed except that he looked contented now. The boredom had always been a pose. They sat down with him, Stephen a bit awkwardly because of his leg.

'My God, Marten! Where on earth did you get that uniform?'

'He looks . . . modishly war-worn,' Mary said. There was a catch in her laugh again.

But right away he found it difficult to make conversation with two people who were trying to behave as if there was nothing going on between them.

'Isn't this like old times? If only Peter . . . ' and she tailed off and looked sad, because in all honesty the last thing they wanted was Peter there.

Stephen looked across at her with quick concern and tried to touch her hand, briefly, but she discreetly moved it. Marten found it strange, because he'd never seen Stephen show that kind of sympathy for another human being before.

'Well, how is poor old Peter?' Stephen asked.

'Why "poor old Peter"?' As soon as he'd said that he regretted it, because it was an unconscious slip by Stephen and there wasn't much point in picking him up on it. Then he had to work hard not to sound disapproving, because he didn't like to see Mary looking unhappy. God knows, there were troubles enough.

So they talked of inconsequential things, carefully avoiding the past or future, or where they all stood in the present. He trotted out the same funny stories about the new pilot making a perfect landing upside down, and the inexperienced Hun who lost his direction and landed at their airfield by mistake.

Then it was time to go. They knew that he knew about them, but wasn't going to say anything. Mary looked weepy and kissed his right cheek.

'Dear Marten, look after yourself . . . and Peter.'

Stephen looked solemn and shook his hand. Then they were gone.

He attended another Medical Board and nobody suggested that he stay in England. His leave had gone flat, and no mistake. But he had to look on the bright side. There was still time for it to get worse. The burning question was what to do with the time remaining.

Already he'd got his orders, and France was beginning to loom large in his waking moments. The days had trickled away like water down the sink. He'd bought his mother a new winter coat with some of his poker winnings, and later he'd seen her through a half-open door, holding the coat and crying softly, as though he were already dead. Then he'd gone to the tailor for another fitting and there was a modest little notice asking for officers to settle their accounts before leaving England. It didn't look as if they were expecting him back from France. One way or another it was a bit depressing, so he went and bought some gramophone records for the squadron mess, and that cheered him up a little. He'd got to start thinking positively, even though the outlook wasn't very promising, so he wrote a letter to Lloyd.

'Dear Lloyd,

I thought they'd killed you, you looked so poorly in the hospital at Hazebrouk. And it wasn't I who talked you into deciding to live. You must have done that for yourself.

As you say, one leg off isn't too bad. In fact

*it might even be an advantage to a raconteur
like yourself.*

*Your letter, redirected several times, caught
up with me in London. I am shortly returning
to the squadron having more or less recovered
from another injury to my face. The left side is
a bit of a mess now, but at least the jaw doesn't
ache any more.*

*In the period between your crash and my
accident, Biggs, Donovan and Drinkwater were
killed, and I hear from Harvey that Lewis has
been invalided home with a nervous
breakdown . . . '*

He paused, frowning down at the paper.

*'. . . so the future looks uncertain for those of
us who are left, and I find it difficult to think
about the end of the war. However, I am
delighted with your news that the Lloyd family
now have virtual control of Baker-Lloyd
Aircraft, and that your profits are so obscenely
high. And I am flattered by your insistence that
I should fly for your company when the war
ends. That's the best offer I've had today!'*

It would be good to fly for a living and have nobody
shooting at you. He finished the letter with more out-of-
date squadron gossip and a promise to visit Lloyd on his
next leave.

The thing was to stop thinking about Jean. He must
start to be more philosophical. After all, with all this
carnage in the world his own small disappointments were
of no real significance. The war was important, and how
men survived and kept their sanity was important, and he
ought to be thinking about that and what it all meant. Yes,

that's what he would do. He'd take a walk in Kensington Gardens and think.

But it was difficult to keep his mind on any one thing. His thoughts moved sharply from cloud cover to the ice on the pond and how the ducks coped with this. How stark the trees looked, and how he'd limped back home that time with three feet of branch caught up in his undercarriage. All his thoughts were small, concerned with himself and his profession, and how to stay alive. The cloud base was pushing down. It must be about two hundred feet. It was funny how he'd not noticed before how efficient the ducks were, breaking their landing speed with their feet. You have a fellow feeling for ducks when you fly yourself. But God, that wind was cold. If it dropped there would be snow. What would it be like flying over the front today? And he must stop looking at every slim, dark girl to see if it was Jean.

The darkness was coming on. How to fill the evening? He could go to one of the officers' clubs in the West End, but he'd tried one or two. Titled ladies offered tea and pleasant conversation to men just like himself, discussing how London had changed, and the possibility of the war ending now that the Americans were arriving in France. On the whole he preferred to be alone, drinking in the anonymous, crowded bar rooms of West London.

There was snow in the air. It was extraordinary the people you met in the pubs of Notting Hill Gate. A crowd of American airmen, just up from Winchester, insisted that he drink with them. They weren't all green. Some of them had flown with the Flying Corps before transferring to the American Army. It got a bit rowdy in the Coach and Horses, with toasts to the Escadrille Lafayette, and toasts to the Flying Corps, then a toast to the American 27th Aero Squadron. And it didn't look as if there would be an end to it, so he resisted an attempt to drag him to a party at

The Grosvenor and lurched off in the direction of home. The collective mindlessness of drinking parties put him off nowadays. The attraction of them was that you didn't have to think.

The wind had dropped and it was just a little warmer. Perhaps he should start to keep a diary. That would force him to concentrate his thoughts. Large pale flakes of snow had begun to drift and side-slip down the air, like white leaves, and soon the pavement was covered and his footfalls muffled.

The inability to concentrate for long on any single thought was in itself quite puzzling. He could note that in his diary. It wasn't just that he had drunk too much, it was the same for many of them even when they were stone cold sober. He'd seen it all the time in France, with men geared up to making fast decisions. It was amazing what a soaring level of adrenalin could do for the thinking processes. But it seemed to be at the cost of sustained thought. One day, when the war was over, there would be a whole generation of men with fast reflexes and a diminished capacity for concentration. Now that was a serious thought. Maybe he could think of a name for that condition, and he would write it in his diary.

He had reached the mews. How tired he was. He'd have to sit on Mrs Payne's dustbin for a few minutes because, in all honesty, he couldn't go in and let his mother see him like this.

He looked at the large luminous dial of his watch. Soon she would be in bed, so for a while he could just sit here and think. He'd got his flask so he could have one last drink to keep out the cold. The snow had a pleasantly lulling effect. A man might fall asleep.

'Come along Marten, up you get.'

A hand was pulling gently at his arm. For God's sake, there was no resting in this world. He said, 'You find your own bloody dustbin.'

'You can't sleep here, Marten. There, good boy, up you get.'

He liked that voice. It was Jean.

'Can't go home yet. Got to think.'

'Thinking is bad for you. Left foot forward, now the right. Splendid.'

'I'm going the wrong way.'

'No you're not.'

'I live over there.'

'Hush now, you'll wake the whole mews up.'

And there he was, stumbling with exaggerated caution up the stairs of Jean's flat. Then, blessed relief, he was lying on a bed, and Jean was hauling him up to pull his tunic off. It was surprising how efficient she was when it came to removing his boots. Even more surprising was his own lack of surprise when she got into bed beside him. It was, after all, the obvious thing to do. Funny how another human being could be so soft in so many places. Her steady breathing made him very sleepy.

The noise of a cart horse clattering out of its stables, slipping on the cobbles, worried him into waking. Then he remembered.

Jean stirred, turning to him, her eyes still closed and her hair falling across her face. He must have slept very soundly because he felt much better now, but how long had he been there? If he held his wrist up he could read the time on the luminous dial of his watch. It was five-thirty. The movement must have woken her.

'Hello Jean,' he said softly.

'Hello Marten. How do you feel now?' She pulled the blankets tight around her neck.

'Much improved, much improved.'

'You'll have to go home soon, before the mews starts to stir.'

'Half an hour perhaps.' He held her breast.

Even in the moonlight he could see she was smiling. Her hand slid up the bare flesh of his side. 'That gives us time.'

He kissed her gently, then moved over onto her; and there was the surprise that is never a surprise. How soft yet firm her body was. Then he was lost.

It was past six o'clock when he surfaced. Jean really did have a cure for tired young heroes. She lay stretched out, smiling but with her eyes closed. 'Go on, off you go.'

He crept out of the flat and crossed the mews. Only old Mr Solomons was about, poking around in the dustbins, then moving on down the mews, talking to himself. The snow had blown into small drifts, pushed up into doorways.

He opened the door very quietly and climbed the stairs, wincing as they creaked. His bed was cold and his feet were frozen. God knows what it would be like, flying over the front next week in this sort of weather. But it didn't matter because right now he felt very calm. Sex on its own didn't have that effect on him; not that he'd had all that much experience of course. There had only been a few hasty bundlings with French girls, and a hurried one-off affair with a major's wife at the flying school.

And now Jean. The whole world looked quite different. So all that nonsense about love turned out to be true after all. But it would do no good to pretend that it was one of the great romances of history, or to become possessive, or to assume that it would last. He must just take each day as it came. After all, in times like these you had to settle for what you could get.

It was, nevertheless, quite flattering that she seemed to have assumed they would be meeting each evening after she'd finished working and had paid a quick call on her sister in Kincaid Street.

169

He waited for her in a small restaurant not far from the hospital. It was odd, that feeling of warmth, knowing she would come yet still finding himself glancing anxiously at the blustery darkness of the winter evening. When she arrived, looking quickly around for him, it seemed she was anxious in the same way.

He couldn't think about tomorrow, because the coming night held such promise. Just seeing her across the restaurant made his hands tremble, and his stomach churned with the same pleasurable sick excitement that she had evoked in him even when he was a schoolboy, doing his homework, glancing through the window, guiltily hoping for a glimpse of her through the half-drawn curtains across the mews. Yet the funny thing was, as soon as she sat opposite him he felt very calm, the way he had on that first morning after he had left her flat.

By some tacit agreement they had not discussed the reason for their bitter scene the night he'd taken her to the concert. And because of the promise he'd made to himself, that he would take each day as it came and not expect too much, he never asked her about the other tired young heroes in her life.

So good was the cure that he could sit quite still, hardly bothering with the brandy the waiter had placed in front of him.

'You smoke too much, it's bad for you.' She touched his nicotine-stained finger.

'It helps me to think,' he said.

'Thinking is bad for you.' She laughed.

He smiled to himself. She'd got it the wrong way round. When times were bad he most wanted to think, yet it was then that the quick surges of adrenalin allowed him only hurried decision. Now that he was calm and relaxed the vaguely-held importance of thinking about his life deserted him.

'No, I don't want you to put the cigarette out, if it helps you.'

He didn't need it. He crushed the cigarette in the ashtray. In fact he smoked much less now. He didn't know how great the need would be next week. 'It's all right,' he said.

He leaned across the table and touched the index finger of her left hand. The nail was broken. All during the day her fingers had been making up medicines, filling in forms, touching her hair, lifting tea cups. And tonight . . .

She smiled lazily at him. 'You've lost a lot of weight, so you must eat more.'

Not much chance of that, with return to the front so near. Fear doesn't make for a healthy appetite. But he turned his head to one side and smiled and nodded.

'And you mustn't keep turning your head away. Though war worn, you are still outrageously handsome.'

That wasn't true, but it didn't matter.

'I remember when I first came to live in the mews.' She paused. 'Let's see, it would have been five years ago. I used to wonder who was the handsome schoolboy who lived opposite.' She frowned slightly. 'I'm three years older than you.'

'Four,' he said, 'but who's counting?'

'Four then.' She smiled down at the table.

Three – four, what did it matter? Time didn't mean very much. It was only how you spent it that mattered.

'If the war hadn't come we would be quite different people, wouldn't we? I would have spent the last three years working in the coal offices.'

'I would probably have moved on, away from the mews,' Jean said.

'And we would not be sitting here now, together.'

'Then something good has come out of the war.'

'I would have filled up my life with small things and

never really learned about myself.'

'And I would have looked for a well-to-do man to marry so that I could live a safe, well-ordered life.'

'We might have met by accident sometimes, and we would have exchanged a few words.'

'Then gone our respective ways with barely a thought about each other.'

'No. I would still have lusted after you, the way I've always done.'

'Did you lust after me when you were a boy?'

'You know I did.'

'Yes, I know you did.'

The next day he got a letter from Peter.

'. . . and although I regret that you will find yourself back on a fairly active section of the front, I will be very pleased to see you. I've missed you. I need your gloomy cynicism to lift my spirits, and as Harvey still cannot find his way unaided from the mess to his quarters, we will all welcome the return of a good navigator.

We are better organised now, and I think you will appreciate this. We have more personnel, better trained, and our accident rate has dropped off.

The short winter days allow for fewer patrols. For my part, I must admit that I am glad of the long nights because I tire so easily now and I need to sleep.

Strange. I thought I saw a yellow-tailed Hun a few days ago, and I had to keep reminding myself, as I reminded you, that there could be several Pfalz scouts with yellow tail fins. Clearly, I have been here too long.

Have you seen Mary while you have been home? I haven't heard from her lately . . . '

He had to stop reading then, because it hurt a bit to think of Peter, tired and war-weary, still waiting for a letter from Mary.

On the morning of Jean's day off they walked in St James' Park and he showed her the ducks, and told her about the way they used their feet to break their landing speed. It was really very clever of them and he would have to write to Lloyd about it, because now that Bristol's were building monoplanes, landing speeds would be higher and the approach flatter. So they really ought to be thinking about fitting some sort of airbrake to aeroplanes. Something that would reduce their speed but not their lift. A section of the wing that could be lowered, perhaps, to increase drag. He was quite lost in thought for a while, wondering how it could be done. Then the bloody rain came on again, and they had to stand together under a tree.

In the afternoon they went to collect his new uniform, and he really had to start thinking about going back to France. He needed a new valise and a writing case. Jean bought him a pair of sheepskin gloves, much better than issue, and a fountain pen to remind him to write to her. He was very touched. They must have cost her a lot, and he hadn't expected anything as expensive as that.

She'd been a bit quiet all day, so in the restaurant that evening he gave her the pendant watch he'd intended saving for her until their last meeting. He talked some nonsense about drinking with Lloyd and Donovan, and Lloyd's obsession with the tubby French girl in the estaminet in Béthune. Then she suddenly said, 'You half want to go back, don't you?'

'No, I don't want to. I have to.' And he felt bad, because that wasn't quite true. And she knew, didn't she, that twice wounded, and with his face like that, and with a DCM to boot, he wouldn't have too much difficulty in getting an instructor's job, or something even safer at home. But why was she asking this? He'd just got used to the idea that he would go back to France and she would probably turn and offer comfort to somebody else. Did he detect some uncertainty in her purpose?

'Why do you have to go?'

Her eyes were on his face, and now he would have to explain the inexplicable.

'It's like some elaborate game that I have to play out to the end. It doesn't have anything to do with who wins the war. If the Medical Board had said that I couldn't go back to France because I was unfit for active service I would have been very relieved. The decision, you see, would have been out of my hands. But as they haven't said that, I'm still in the game.'

'A game!' She looked puzzled and a little impatient. 'Do you mean that there are rules?'

'Yes,' he said. And the sudden sharp image of Yellow Tail raking Benge's machine made him bite his lip and frown. 'There are rules of a sort, though sometimes they're hard to follow.'

'You mean you have some sort of warriors' code?' She looked sceptical.

'No. To have a warriors' code would mean that I had fairly precise terms of reference. All that I ever had was a bundle of compromises and a few loyalties. There are certain rules observed by the others, but I couldn't always accept them. Sometimes I couldn't even recognise them because my rag-bag collection of values kept getting in the way.' He frowned to himself, groping with the question that still nagged sometimes. Would it have made any difference if he had stayed with Drinkwater and Donovan that day, instead of going back to look for Harvey?

'How can you stay in the game if you can't even recognise the rules?'

174

'Perhaps I'll recognise them when I go back.'

She looked at him steadily for a moment. It was very disconcerting the way she did that. Then she said, 'And what is the object of the game?'

'I'm not sure.' And that was the truth. 'They try to make us into machines; but we're not machines.' After nearly four years of kill or be killed, the cause meant nothing to him. 'I don't know if the object is to stick by Peter, Harvey, Smith and the others. Or if it's to beat the game by still being on my feet at the end.'

For the first time since he'd known her she looked startled, like a confident navigator who suddenly realises that the maps no longer quite relate to the landscape. Then she looked down at the table. 'Do I have any place in your game?'

He could feel his face screwing up in a frown because he was on very unsafe ground. In all honesty he and she had been playing a game as well, nicely circumscribed, with implied rules and assumptions. And by probing, to see if he would of his own free will leave her to go to France, she had extended the game's dimensions.

'I suppose it depends on how far we want to get involved,' he said.

So they sat there in silence for a while, because he knew, and she knew too, that to get farther involved meant commitment, and there was nothing easy about making that kind of leap in times like these. Then they did what was safe and talked about other things. But the unspoken question of what was to become of them lay between them for the last two days.

Then there was only one more night left. She hadn't wanted to go anywhere and they had supper in her flat. He lay on his back, tired from making love, and she lay curled up next to him, and the coal fire cast moving shadows on the walls and ceiling.

Even accepting that they were not committed to each other, he felt he ought to tell her how important she was to him.

'Jean?' he whispered, though he didn't know why.

'Yes?' The word was muffled because her mouth was pressed against his side.

'I've been thinking about us.'

She laughed softly. 'Thinking is bad for you.'

'When I came home I was like a dead man.'

She stirred and leaned up on her elbow, and her breast lay on his shoulder as she looked down at him.

'When we started,' he said, 'I couldn't think about later, to here and now, and you and me together. You were wiser. You said I would complicate your life, and perhaps I have. But I feel alive again.'

'Hush.' Her fingers stroked the scars on his face. 'We don't have to talk about it.'

'I'll tell you anyway. Because you've made me feel alive again I don't assume that you feel committed to me.'

She sat up, with her arms clasped around her knees and the firelight on her bare shoulders.

'I don't know,' she said. 'I don't know if I am committed to you. I won't know that until after you've gone away from me.' She sighed. 'I knew that I'd care about somebody again one day, but I never dreamed it would be you. I suppose I'll dread the postman coming, or not coming. And I'll not sleep well. And I'll wake up thinking of you.'

'Thinking is bad for you,' he said, and drew her down next to him. They lay quite still, staring up at the moving shadows on the ceiling.

The clock at St Stephen's Church chimed midnight, and then it was the day that he was to go back.

Eleven

KILLER SMITH was in the squadron office when he arrived back. Almost as if he'd been waiting for him.

'They haven't done a bad job on you, considering what you looked like when we pulled you out of that wreck,' he said, examining him critically. 'Mind you, you're still a bloody mess.'

'Thank you so much,' he said.

'What are comrades for?' Smith grinned and shrugged. 'I'm puzzled, Corby. I mean, with your face like that, you could have got out. Gone back to civilian life bearing the honourable scars of war.'

'I had to get back to you, Killer. You're a prince among men.'

'No. Don't bother about carrying your bags. We'll get one of these lazy sods to carry them.' Smith called to an orderly. 'Get up off your backside and take the lieutenant's bags over to Mr Harvey's hut.' And he turned back to him. 'Come on, Corby. I'll walk some of the way with you. I asked the new recording officer to put you in with Harvey, you and him being mates.'

This wasn't the way he remembered Smith at all. But everything seemed to have changed. Most of the tents had gone, replaced by snug Nissen huts all neat and orderly, so at least he wouldn't die of pneumonia. And there were concrete paths between the smart new wooden buildings adjoining the abandoned flour mill. Some diligent souls had even attempted small garden plots alongside their living quarters.

'New mess hut.' Smith nodded towards a long, low

wooden building. 'We got it up in time for Christmas.'

'Any beams for you to swing on?'

'I don't go in there much, except for breakfast and lunch,' Smith said.

What had come over the fellow? Smith had been the life and soul of the mess, back in the old days. So he asked him. 'What do you do with your evenings, then?'

'Oh, I go into Amiens usually.' Smith was frowning, preoccupied with his thoughts. 'I feel like a stranger in that mess sometimes. We've got some good kids in with us now. You'll see. They're better trained than we were. But they're still kids. Nearly all the old hands have gone. You hear about Lewis and his nervous breakdown?'

'I heard he'd been sent home.'

The Killer looked contemptuous. 'Well, Lewis was always a bit gutless. Templer used to prop him up all the time. And after Templer was killed he just went to pieces. Got in his machine one day and flew north-west till he ran out of fuel and landed in a potato patch near Boulogne. A colonel turned up in a big car, to find out what he was doing there. And Lewis looked at the red staff tabs on the colonel's collar and said, 'Christ! I didn't know I'd got so far from the fighting!'

Marten felt his face cracking in a crooked grin.

Smith went on, 'So they didn't know whether to charge him with insulting behaviour or desertion, or both. But Peter got him off the hook. Said that Lewis had been on the brink of a nervous breakdown. And Lewis played along with it, so they sent him home.' Smith shrugged. 'If it had been me, I would have had the bastard shot.'

'What about the others?'

'Zac Turner keeled over one day. But what could you expect with his guts in that state? They rushed him off to hospital. He'll be all right, but he won't be coming back to France. You know about Stansfield? A social disease, as

178

they say in polite society. One too many of those French whores. He was always a randy sod. And as a replacement we've got a smart-alec kid in as commander of A Flight. Name of Carson. They call him Kit. It's a joke, see? You'll know him when you see him. Looks about sixteen with a face like a baby, and an MC and a bloody Belgian Croix de Guerre. Of course, old Carver still commands B Flight, but he should be going home for good soon. He's had enough. He would have gone ages ago if they'd got a replacement for him. That's the problem. We've got all these keen young kids, but there aren't enough experienced flight commanders to go round. So they can send people like Roper home, but they've had to keep Carver out here.'

'What happened to Roper? Did he finally succumb to his piles?'

Smith looked gloomy and shrugged again. 'I dunno. He's gone though. And we've got a granite-faced bastard called McGraw as recording officer. Bloody balloonist! What the hell does he know about aeroplanes?'

'I take it you don't like him?'

'He's too efficient. This squadron isn't what it used to be. Granted, we used to be a bit sloppy, but we got things done one way or another.' Smith indicated with disgust the overalled men busy painting the outside walls of the armament store. 'All bloody paint, and forms in triplicate. I tell you, Corby, it's hardly worth shooting down a Hun, it creates so much paper work.'

He slowed his pace outside a long Nissen hut. 'That's your quarters. You share the third cubicle with Harvey, and a kid named St John.' Smith nodded, and paused, as if he had something else to say but didn't know quite how to say it.

Marten had delayed asking the question, but as Smith was so affable he decided to put it to him casually. 'Who am I flying with?'

Smith frowned down at the ground, as if embarrassed. 'You fly with me. And I've got to say this, Corby, because it's been on my mind. I don't know what your attitude to the war is now, but you've got a lot of backbone, coming back here, with your face like that.'

'I didn't have much choice. They just sent me.'

'Yeh.' But Smith didn't believe it. 'That kid, St John, picked up a new SE for you yesterday. You can try it out this afternoon. We'll go over the front together tomorrow.'

He stood and watched Smith slouching away, his long arms swinging ape-like and his head jutting aggressively forward. It was hard to understand the Killer.

But he needed some practice with the new SE, after all those weeks in England. The truth was, he couldn't wait to fly again because he had to find out if he'd lost his touch.

There was nobody in the cubicle. He searched around in Harvey's locker and found a helmet and goggles, and went over to the C Flight hangars.

The mechanics manhandled his new machine out onto grass while he tested the ground with the heel of his boot. It was soggy. He glanced around. Who picked these God-awful fields? Over there, around the middle. That was where he'd crashed. He frowned and whistled to himself, then climbed up into the cockpit. Would it be like learning to fly all over again?

Everything worked. The engine started first time and the young mechanic stood back waiting for him to go, so there was no putting it off. The SE pounded over the uneven surface of the wet field and he could barely read the vibrating instruments. At sixty-five miles an hour the tail came up. At seventy-five the wheels lifted and the pounding ceased as he climbed steadily into the grey sky.

He kept going up until the earth was a brown-green

sameness below him, then he levelled out. The machine moved smoothly through the still air.

His nervousness eased. But the confidence wasn't there yet. And it wouldn't be, until every small movement of his hands and feet gave him a predicted response. At first his slight pressures on the control stick and rudder bar were tentative, exploratory, then instinct took over once more.

He opened the throttle until the air speed read one hundred and thirty, and pulled the nose up vertically towards the watery sun. The controls went soft as he reached the top of the loop, then he dropped nose downwards again.

He timed himself on a slow roll. It took him eight seconds. The machine would flick roll easily to the right but only clumsily to the left, and no matter what he did he couldn't improve it. So he'd remember that tomorrow. Now he felt almost at ease. He spun first to the left and then to the right. He hadn't lost his touch.

When he landed, Harvey was waiting for him. And he only faltered for a second when he saw his face, then pounded him on the back.

'The minute you get back you get into a cockpit again.'

'I had to see if I could still do it.'

'You land with style. I've been telling these guys what a hot pilot you are. Come on back to the hut and meet our latest cell mate.'

'I will soon. I'd better go and sign for this machine. Is Peter around?'

'I don't think so. He's at a big-deal meeting at Wing HQ. But you'll have to see Mighty McGraw first anyway. We go through channels these days.'

Marten had a feeling he wasn't going to like McGraw. McGraw had a system for everything and all new arrivals were supposed to see him before they did anything else. It was a bit off-putting to be kept waiting like this, when in the old days he'd have just strolled into the admin building and put his head round Peter's door.

Captain McGraw looked old and tough, and too big for the chair and desk. His grey hair was cut very short and his moustache measured exactly the width of his upper lip. There was perhaps a regulation about it somewhere. You could see he was efficient because his desk was nearly clear of rubbish. Old Roper used to keep just about everything on the desk, cluttered up among the newspapers and empty tea mugs.

'Ah. You're Corby, aren't you?' McGraw's clear blue eyes rested for just a moment on the damaged half of his face. 'We'd better get your documentation up to date. Sit down. I won't keep you long.' He began filling in some forms, assigning him to a hut and allocating him an aeroplane. 'It's a new machine, ferried over from the depot yesterday, so you should have no problems.'

'Yes. I've flown it already. It's fine.'

'Oh.' McGraw looked vexed. 'You shouldn't have done that. You haven't signed for the machine.' He sighed. 'It is important that we do things properly.'

'I'm sorry.' Though he couldn't imagine why he should be. 'I'm flying with the Killer tomorrow and I wanted to get a good hour of practice in this afternoon.'

'You mean Captain Smith. Understandable. But you should have looked in first. Never mind now. If you take this chit to the stores people you can pick up your flying clothes and a time-piece. And I see you had a revolver booked out to you but lost it when you crashed at – let's see – Poelkapelle. And you were given another one which was also lost when you last crashed?'

'That's right.' He didn't feel like explaining.

McGraw waited for a second, then grunted and

nodded. 'You'll need one then. I know Major West is anxious to see you. Try and catch him tomorrow.' The blue eyes rested on his face again. 'If there is anything I can do to help you settle back in, don't hesitate to let me know.'

So maybe Mighty McGraw wasn't such a bad chap after all. But of course, he wasn't a pilot.

It wasn't until the next day, when he was flying over the front with Smith, and feeling very nervous, that he began to see the significance of the tentatively optimistic comments he'd heard in the mess. They'd got more planes on the sector now. He could see a whole squadron of F2b's off to the left, formidable and dark against the pale clouds, and two flights of Camels coming back from patrol. And either Smith was feeling a bit off today, or he'd become less hell-bent on winning the war on his own. There were some Huns a good way off, but when he signalled, the Killer just nodded and stayed on course.

'The Killer seems very relaxed these days,' he said to Harvey, when they returned.

'He's got himself a well-to-do French widow. Husband killed at Neuve Chapelle. Baker found out about it.'

'I miss all the scandal now Lewis is no longer with us. What about Smith's wife?'

'She's probably shacked up with his brother. Anyway, Smith doesn't seem to care about her little indiscretions any more.'

'Lewis always maintained that Smith was impotent. Perhaps the widow lady has changed all that.'

'*Vive la veuve.* Let's hope that his bitchy wife leaves him alone. For all our sakes.'

Killer Smith and Kit Carson tried to get him to play poker, but he wouldn't. He knew, without even sitting in on a game, that his long run of card luck was over. It had always worried him, winning like that. He hadn't enjoyed being that different, waiting for his comeuppance.

Well, he'd had a comeuppance. And now he could ease his way among the newcomers; one of them, yet acceptably detached from them because of his face. The old feelings of guilt and indecision had faded, as had the pain in his jaw. Now he just did his job, fairly thoroughly but no more than that, and didn't concern himself with reasons why he was here. It was almost as if, by having his face smashed up, he'd expiated all his sins, of design or omission, imagined or real. If his luck held, he'd just scrape along until the war ended. That was all he wanted to do. On his fourth day back he shot down an Albatross and felt no qualms. In fact he felt a bit better. As if he'd made up for the one who got Benge.

Peter had changed. No doubt about that. He was different. He still had the appearance of a young mercenary prince, but he was weary, as if he'd fought one campaign too many.

'Tell me about yourself, Marten.' Peter leaned back in the old swivel chair, frowning attentively. 'They fixed you up, did they, as best they could?'

'Yes. My jaw doesn't hurt any more.'

'And does the damage to your face worry you?'

'A bit. Not too much.'

'Splendid.'

What was Peter really thinking?

'Did you see Mary while you were home? I haven't heard from her for a week or more.'

'Yes, I did see her.'

Peter waited for him to say more, but he couldn't bring himself to mention that Stephen had been with her, and merely added, 'She seemed very well.'

'God! This bloody war does drag on, doesn't it?' Peter lit a cigarette, frowning. 'We would have got married if I'd accepted that Home Establishment posting. I wonder now

184

if I did the right thing.' He chewed on his thumbnail and looked concerned.

'Don't worry about it now,' he said, because he didn't like to see Peter so uncertain. 'It will all end soon. Two hundred and fifty thousand American soldiers are landing in France each month. The Huns will give up. And we'll go home together.'

'Yes, that's right. We'll go home together.' Peter smiled. 'And what will we do, Marten?'

'I don't know. But we'll do *something*.' The trouble was, he just couldn't see it. Peter seemed fixed here, as permanently as the image on a photograph.'Do you know, some Frenchman named Orteig has offered a prize of twenty-five thousand dollars for the first men to fly non-stop between New York and Paris. Maybe we'll have a go at that. It couldn't be any more dangerous than flying over the front day after day.'

Peter grinned ruefully and rubbed his hand over his jaw. 'You know that Richthofen has four squadrons operating in our area? I fear that something big is brewing.'

Peter wasn't the only one who thought that. Along with all the optimism about the Americans arriving in large numbers, there was a growing feeling that Ludendorff would have one last go before the summer came. Harvey seemed sure of it, and said he would like to see Paris again, because if the Huns were going to start something, it might be months before he could take another visit.

'Why is it that Paris has such a fascination for Americans?' St John asked as they got up for early breakfast. 'Is it the high class French whores?'

'Hell no!' Harvey shook his head. 'It's because Paris is the artistic, literary and intellectual capital of the world. My dad brought my mother over, for the Exhibition of 1889. Last time I was in Paris I tried to go to all the places they went to, but I only had a couple of days. I visited the Louvre. Did you know that all contemporary American art derives its influence from Paris?' He sighed. 'I'd sure like to go there again.'

So he said, 'I'll tell you what we'll do, Harvey. We'll fly down into the French sector and see if we can get just a glimpse of the artistic, literary and intellectual capital of the world.'

'Hey! That's a great idea.'

'I don't know why you bother,' St John said. 'Don't all good Americans go to Paris when they die? Harvey will be going there soon anyway, in spirit at least.'

The opportunity came two days later. He and Harvey flew south to the suburbs of Paris. They were close enough to see the Eiffel Tower stretching up, its top nearly as high as they were, and Notre Dame jutting up from the Ile de la Cité, and the pale sunlight reflecting off the river with its thirty bridges. Then they turned back.

They'd got as far as the Oise again. He was just thinking how odd it was that they hadn't seen any French aeroplanes, when three Nieuport scouts climbed up from below. But their markings were wrong. The roundels on their wings were white in the centre, then blue, then red.

Now the three were close, flying alongside him and Harvey, and he could see the insignia on the fuselage of each machine, just aft of the cockpits. It was a top hat inside a circle. Harvey was waving frantically to get his attention, and his lips moved, exaggerating each word. 'THEY'RE AMERICANS.'

Of course they bloody were! Now he understood the significance of the insignia. Those Americans, flying French machines, and probably with English fuel in their tanks, had thrown their hats into the ring. So things were looking up.

'94th Aero Squadron,' Harvey said when they got

back. 'The first at the front. You see, there will be hundreds of them over here soon.'

Kit Carson thought it was a pity that the Americans would arrive in large numbers and end the war before he had managed to establish himself as an ace. He coughed hugely into his handkerchief.

'Kit, you ought to do something about that cough of yours,' Smith said. 'You're beginning to make me feel quite ill.'

'I thought a nice little jaunt in the early morning might shift it.' Carson gasped for breath then coughed again. 'What do you say to the idea of you, me and Corby trying a dawn raid on Richthofen's field at Douai? Corby's a good navigator. He could get us there at first light.'

'For God's sake!' The boy wonder was even madder than he'd thought. 'No thank you,' he said. 'I'm hoping to get through the rest of this war with what's left of me intact.'

Surprisingly Smith agreed with him. 'I'm getting too old for that sort of thing, Kit.'

Carson cajoled between bouts of coughing. 'Oh, come on, Killer. I thought I could count on you. You've got a reputation to live up to. Twelve Huns downed. And Steiner. The people back home expect it of you.'

'Stuff the people back home,' Smith said savagely. 'There's nothing for me back there. I'm staying in France when it's all over. Above ground if possible.'

There was a trace of superiority in Carson's smile. 'The widow in Amiens?'

'That's right. My Brigitte may not be a beauty, but she treats me well. And she's got a small machine tool factory, left her by her husband. It's a bit run-down but I'll turn it into something. I'm going to marry that lady and I'm going to get rich and fat.'

Carson's boyish charm had turned a bit hard. 'And

you, Corby. Are you contemplating a boring, bourgeois future?'

'I'm hoping for *a* future, Kit. I have every intention of jogging along until I've served out my time. I'll leave the heroism to you.'

And if he just did an honest job, and no more, he could still feel that he wasn't letting anybody down, and he was keeping his word to Jean. He wasn't deliberately squandering what she offered.

On that morning, the day he'd returned to France, she'd come to the station with him. He'd known it would be difficult, but she'd wanted it that way. They'd found him a seat in a carriage already occupied by three officers, then stood on the platform by the open carriage door, jostled by soldiers burdened with kit bags and rifles, and their relatives and loved ones determinedly cheerful until the last minute.

He attempted conversation about the journey, and how he would write to her by the next evening. She was pale, and yes, she was beautiful. He told her so.

'Witchcraft.' She smiled and the long eye teeth showed.

He felt guilty. How could he leave her, for France and the war, and a bundle of misguided notions of responsibility?

He started to say how much he would miss her, but the engine whistle shrieked and she pressed her hands to her ears to shut out the harsh sound.

'Jean,' he said. He was going to try and say all those things he wanted to be true; that his luck would hold, that he would come back, that it would be good again.

She took her hands from her ears, and placed her fingers on his lips. 'Don't squander it,' she said. The guard blew his whistle and carriage doors were slamming. He hugged her quickly and climbed into the carriage. She stood, tall and slim among the press of people on the platform. As the train curved away she raised her hand very slightly then let it fall. He watched her until his view was obscured by girders and stonework.

He'd half expected her to offer her cure to someone else. It would have been fair for her to turn elsewhere because they'd made no promises. But it didn't seem to have happened, yet. She wrote to him twice a week; about the hospital and the mews, and about her widowed sister in Kincaid Street. And she always ended her letters with how much she missed him, face and all. Up to now she had made no mention of the future, and neither had he. But that was probably wise of them both, because maybe there was no future. All along the front men had begun to brace themselves, not knowing where or when the storm would come, only that it would come. And when it came it would snuff out lives held precariously, like candles in a wind. Even if the war dragged on only until late summer, many would fall down the sky before it ended.

Twelve

NOBODY SEEMED to know what was happening. A thickening haze had descended. It was like being in a white sea. Mist swirled over the huts and between them. Sometimes Marten could see the corner of the admin building, then it disappeared again. Even the insistent thudding of the distant artillery seemed muted now by the rolling vapour. They had breakfasted and, dressed ready to fly, they stood in groups in hut doorways, their conversation subdued. And they waited for news.

McGraw kept coming out from the admin building, peering round at the impossible weather, then going back to the telephone. It was no good Wing phoning up every five minutes to ask why they weren't over the front. They could do nothing in mist like this. Every now and then new and frightening rumours circulated. The whole of the front, from Ypres to La Fère, had been smashed by shellfire and saturated with gas.

Every twenty minutes Marten got up into his cockpit and ran up the engine to keep it warm, and the others started to do the same. But he was getting very chilled, hanging about like this and nervous anxiety had begun to eat into him. So he got Harvey and they went over to the office and stood by the stove.

McGraw, less formal now that the battle had begun, held the mouthpiece of the telephone to his chest and bawled to the duty clerk to fetch them all some tea. Then he went back to his long-distance conversation.

'Would you say that again? This line is bad.'

The clerk brought in three mugs of tea.

'What's happening?' Harvey was impatient to know.

McGraw waved his hand to shut Harvey up. Then nodded, frowning at the wall as he listened to the voice at the other end of the line.

'The whole front, you say. And they are shelling St Pol. What the hell are they shelling St Pol for? It's twenty miles behind the line.'

'Railway junction,' Marten said. But McGraw wasn't listening so he went back to sipping his tea and muted conversation with Harvey.

Smith and Carver came in and stood by the stove. Smith rubbed his hands to warm them.

'Where's Peter?'

McGraw pointed to the squadron commander's door and turned his attention to the phone again.

Carver went to look at the map on the wall. It was curling at one corner. There were coloured pencil marks all over it and a thick dotted line from top left to bottom right, indicating the front. The dotted line had been erased inexpertly and altered to take in the Cambrai Salient. They'd be altering it again before this day was out.

McGraw's voice was rising. 'What did you say! They're shelling Paris!'

Peter appeared briefly from his office. 'The Huns have smashed through the line. They've driven a wedge between the third and fifth Armies.'

No doubt about it. It was going to be a big one.

He and Harvey went out to run up their engines again, and he suddenly noticed that he could see all the hangars and even beyond. At the same moment the klaxon sounded, da dit da dit, for C Flight to prepare for take-off. So he took a deep breath and started to strap himself into the cockpit. Smith was running across the cinders, with Tanner, Powell and St John just behind him. Then the klaxon sounded again to alert B Flight, so they'd have eleven machines over the front in fifteen minutes.

Though maybe there was no front now, the Huns were moving so fast. They advanced in a ragged line abreast, through the thinning mist.

You'd have thought three times over would be enough for one day. He came back after the third sortie with half the fabric torn off his lower port wing. Peter was standing there in his flying kit, waiting, and pointing to the spare machine as he taxied towards the hangars. So he went out again.

After the fourth flight, well into the afternoon, even the Killer was complaining. 'For Christ's sake! We've been in the air nearly eight hours today.'

The light had faded and there was the possibility that they'd shot at retreating British infantry by mistake. Carson was leaning up against his fuselage, coughing. 'Dammit,' he said, and gasped. 'I didn't know what I was shooting at.'

Smith waved his hand wearily. 'Can't be helped. And say, Corby, thanks for drawing off some of that ground fire. Do you hear that, Tanner? It confuses the bastards when they have two targets to shoot at. It's no good you sticking right behind me.'

Tanner looked contrite. 'I'm sorry, sir. But you said to stick close.'

'Yes, quite.' Smith looked impatient. 'But you have to use your loaf. I don't want your propeller up my backside. Watch how Corby and Harvey work together. You bloody kids have a lot to learn if you're going to stay alive through this campaign. Much worse, you might get me killed, and that would be unforgivable.'

Peter had flown with them on the last close support flight and he was a bit frosty with Smith.

'You could have pressed harder. We're not going to stop them this way. The infantry need all the help they can get.'

Smith snarled, 'I've done my share today. You're not going to bury me!'

Peter looked at him steadily, then smiled. 'Of course you did. I'm sorry, Killer.' He put his hand on Smith's shoulder. 'I'm a bit keyed up. Go and get something to eat. I'll see to everything here.'

Peter watched, puzzled, as Smith shambled off towards the huts. He'd always been sure of Smith, until now. And all this must be doubly hard for him because he'd finally got the letter from Mary.

Marten knew about the letter because Mary had written to him as well, saying that she and Stephen were engaged to be married, and would he look after Peter as she knew how upset he would be. Dammit, why had she picked a time like this? And why had she involved him? He'd got enough to worry about, just staying alive.

He tried to see Peter, but McGraw was in there with Price, and the technical sergeant major. Peter looked very harassed. 'I'm sorry, Marten. Could you come back some other time? We have to go over the requirements for tomorrow.' As he turned to go they'd all got their heads down again, and Peter was saying they might get some squadrons in from other parts of the front.

But it was going to take more than a handful of planes to stem the advancing tide. Ludendorff's 2nd Army pushed up from St Quentin to Peronne. Soon the Kaiser would be joining them for breakfast. The Cambrai Salient had been squeezed out, so all that fighting the previous autumn had been for nothing. The whole of the British VII Corps had broken and run. The Huns captured Bapaume, and Albert fell two days later. Group Headquarters had lost count of how many German squadrons were in the area. Kit Carson went out coughing to his machine and shot down two Pfalz scouts on the last day of the financial year. 'To even up the books,' he said. But it was a drop in the bucket.

Then it was the First of April, 1918, and the Royal Flying Corps ceased to exist. They became the Royal Air Force, and somebody should have picked a better day for it. There were twenty German divisions astride the Somme. They were only eleven miles from Amiens, and Carver, who was finally going home for good on the twenty-fifth of the month, said that if Amiens fell they could lose the war.

Lose the war! It didn't seem possible.

Peter had started filling in again until replacements arrived. It worked out that on some days he was flying more than the rest of them. It was a bit odd, and slightly frightening. Peter might not be enjoying it, but it was satisfying him in some perverse way. The earlier Smith syndrome, perhaps? Who could tell what was going on inside another man's head?

Then Carver ploughed his SE into the field. It took four of them to get him out of the wreck. Carver kept saying, 'Bloody silly thing to do,' before they got him onto the stretcher and he finally passed out.

'Both legs broken in several places, but they are repairable,' Peter said later.

You couldn't complain about that. But it was hard luck to crash just a few days before going home for good.

Marten lit a cigarette and stared out of the office window. Old Carver was well out of the war. No more crawling out at dawn to a freezing cockpit and the prospect of death before a decent breakfast.

'You'll have to lead B Flight,' Peter said.

He had a sudden fit of coughing. 'Me! You mean until they send somebody to take Carver's place?'

'No. Permanent. I've been onto Wing. There's no immediate prospect of a replacement being posted in. It seems that we still have a shortage. So you've been promoted to the rank of captain. Congratulations.'

194

He didn't want to be a captain. Didn't he have some choice in the matter?

'Peter, I don't really see myself in this role. Couldn't you promote somebody else?'

Peter fell back in his chair and looked weary. 'Like who, for instance? I've got nobody else anywhere near as good as you. And Carson has to have a medical examination at Etaples, so that will leave us without a leader for A Flight for a day or two at least. I'll have to take that on. Don't let me down.' He stared up expectantly. 'You've led patrols before. You'll manage perfectly well.'

He felt trapped. 'What's wrong with Carson? Look, all I want to do is serve out my time until the war ends. I'm not a leader.'

'Good god, man! You've heard his bloody cough.' He has to have a check-up. And if we only promoted born leaders there wouldn't be enough flight commanders to go round, or squadron commanders, or bloody generals for that matter. We take the most experienced men we've got and we use them as best we can.'

'What about Baker? He's not bad.'

'No. You're my best bet at this moment. I'm not asking you to take command of the Royal Air Force. I'm just asking you to lead six machines.' Peter leaned forward in the old swivel chair and waited for an answer.

But it wasn't just a matter of flying in front of five other machines. There was more to it than that, as well he knew. And now he'd got the same old problem, of trying to juggle the demands of responsibility and self-respect against the safer course, of simply doing his fair share and no more. So he sat there, uncertain, and angry, though he didn't know whom to direct his anger against.

Peter watched his face carefully. 'The last big battle of the war, Marten. It can't go on for much longer. But you can see how I'm placed. Smith is holding back on me, he's getting too careful, and Carver's gone, and Kit Carson's sick. I can't do it all on my own.'

No, obviously he couldn't. Squadron commanders weren't supposed to fly over the front, and there was Peter taking on more patrols than any of them. Even so, Marten hadn't come back to France with his face smashed up just to win the war for everybody.

But there wasn't really a choice. He would have to accept. Wasn't it always the way? You took up a position, then people or circumstances ruined it for you. He'd conceded that he must pull his weight, and inevitably his contribution had escalated.

He sighed. 'Right.'

Peter leaned back in his chair, still looking searchingly into his face. 'Good,' he said. 'Cheer up, Marten. I have every confidence in you. And a flight of your own will give you a great opportunity. I need your best effort, to see us through the next few weeks.'

He nodded. A great opportunity to give himself completely to the war. Jean had said he would do all that they asked of him. She'd probably known all along how he would react when he got back here. The thought was depressing, that he could be so predictable, despite his honest protests. Lewis was the only one of them who had rejected the great hustle, made his own decisions, got out. And all that time ago it had been Lewis who had said they were each of them carried along on the tide of circumstance.

'We must celebrate your promotion,' Peter said, and took the bottle and glasses from his drawer. 'Why, with me leading and you behind me, we'll win the war between us.' He grinned. 'Or go down trying.'

Go down trying. Yes, that seemed likely with Peter in his present state. So he would be a hero after all. But Jean had said, impassioned, that it was better to live. And she was right.

He knew now that, with added responsibility, he must keep survival in the front of his thoughts. He must draw a line. And in that grey area where duty blurred into self-sacrifice, he must know which side of the line he was on. It might mean holding back, the way Smith was now doing, but that was the way it had to be. Where did that leave Peter? Alone. It was the first time he'd ever consciously acknowledged that there might be a limit to his support for Peter, and he felt like Judas.

'Here's to us, Marten.' Peter raised his glass. 'And the last battles of the war.'

Peter was like a man deliberately preparing for a hazardous journey, unaware that his companion was already making contingency plans for desertion. Maybe the great test of friendship would never come. But again, maybe it would. So he would have to tell him. He'd always known that Peter was vulnerable. Now he knew why.

'I'll do as you ask, Peter. I'll lead the flight and I'll do as good a job as I can. But I'm not going to die for the war if I can possibly help it. I've drawn a line, here in my head. This far but no further.'

Peter knew exactly what he meant. He didn't say anything for a moment. There was the same puzzled expression on his face that he'd seen there the day Smith had vehemently declared that he wasn't going to let Peter bury him. The same day that Mary had sent the letter saying she was going to marry Stephen.

Peter raised his glass and swallowed down the amber liquid in one gulp. As if he were drinking to something now gone.

Was this how friendship ended? Would it have been better never to have acknowledged a limit?

'Fair enough, Marten,' he said.

And that was all.

They had a modest little party in the mess, to celebrate his promotion, and the bar to Smith's Military Cross. Marten drank too much for the first time in weeks. Smith had foregone his visit to his widow, now evacuated to Abbeville. He seemed depressed and he too was drinking with deliberation. Kit Carson proposed a toast, 'To Captain Corby,' then went back to coughing into his handkerchief.

Baker was punishing the worn-out piano and one of the replacements sang in a fine tenor voice, *Keep The Home Fires Burning*. There was a sadness in it that made them all pause.

'For God's sake!' Smith bawled. He was in a black mood. 'We're supposed to be celebrating. Give us *The Landlady's Daughter*.'

The young replacement obliged and they all joined in the alternate lines.

Marten wasn't enjoying it. Not one bit. And he was keeping out of Peter's way, up there at the end of the bar, because he felt a growing sense of guilt. No good to reason that he shouldn't feel this way, that twice wounded was enough. Could these ugly scars on his face ever justify what he'd done?

A group of the younger pilots had begun swinging on the beams. Few remembered that Smith had invented the game. The biggest of them swung nearly the length of the hut before crashing down, and overturning a table in a welter of broken glasses.

The mess door swung open, letting in the chill clean air, and McGraw entered, pushing his way towards Peter at the end of the bar. His hurried movement and momentary loss of composure caught the attention of Baker, who paused, hands poised over the keys of the piano. The young replacement sang another line of *The Landlady's Daughter*, then tailed off. Beam-swinging ceased and the group turned expectantly towards the bar.

McGraw spoke briefly to Peter. Peter's expression didn't change. He banged his fist on a table to silence lingering conversations.

'Gentlemen. Richthofen has been shot down and killed.'

Everybody began shouting at once. It didn't seem possible. Who would have thought that the ace of aces would go down?

Somebody proposed a toast to the Red Baron and they all solemnly drank.

By God, he was drunk! It was an odd sensation, repeating the half-forgotten toast to Steiner, all those months ago. Then, Smith had been flushed with triumph. Now he just looked cynical. But then, Smith had more in common with Richthofen than with the excited young hopefuls in their new, bright blue uniforms.

Peter looked wearily indifferent, standing alone now, apparently oblivious to the noise around him.

So he couldn't leave it like that. He'd have to go and talk to Peter, that was, if he could reach the bar without falling over.

He leaned against the bar because the mess appeared to be spinning slowly round.

'Peter, I'm sorry. We're still friends?'

'Of course we are. Don't worry about it.'

'We'll still see the war out together. And we'll go home?'

'Yes. Good fellow. Don't drink any more.' Peter put his hand out and held his shoulder. 'Go and get some sleep.'

He rubbed his hands over the scars on his face. Yes. Sleep. That was what he needed.

'I'll see you in the morning.' The mess was spinning in the opposite direction now. 'You get some sleep too. And we'll be all right, won't we?'

'Yes. We'll be all right.'

'And we're still friends?'

'Yes, we're still friends.'

'Goodnight then, friend.'

'Goodnight.'

Thirteen

THE FINE RAIN AND MIST obscured his vision. He had to get the squadron back into some semblance of order. He moved up behind Peter's crippled machine, then waved to Harvey and Baker, signalling that they should form up in echelon on his right and left. And one by one the others tagged on, in a straggling vee, each of them waiting for his signals. Peter lurched on ahead, his SE wallowing like a drunken cow.

Ahead and off to the left a sinister yellowish cloud of gas mingled with the mist swirling over the fretted, red-brick ruins on the summit at Villers-Bretonneux, captured by the enemy that morning. Now there was nothing but a westward stream of wounded between them and Amiens.

Bits were falling off the tail of Peter's machine. He was losing height. But there was a chance for him, there, where Richthofen had crashed last Sunday, on the high slopes just before the Ancre joined the Somme. The Australian 5th Division held that high ground. Peter was too low now to clear it. He'd glanced back briefly and raised his hand.

Soldiers were running along the slope, out of the path of the sinking machine. Peter's helmeted head was tilted sideways as the SE crunched onto the surface of the slope and slithered to a halt.

He'd followed Peter, losing height behind him, and for a fraction of time, burned into his mind, he saw Peter sitting quite still, upright in the cockpit as an orange flame erupted from the main tank behind the engine. Then the gravity tank in the wing exploded.

He couldn't take it in. He hauled up the nose of his SE, climbing through the column of black, oily smoke rising from the wreck. No time to think about it. There was no Smith to lead them. And no Peter.

Dear God, why did you do it, Peter? I was not so good a friend.

McGraw was out there, waiting for them, his greatcoat collar turned up and his hands sunk deep in his pockets, counting them as they came back.

'Where's the major? And Smith! There are four missing!'

He stayed, sitting in the cockpit for a moment, too weary to move.

'The major is dead.' He pulled his goggles off and rubbed the rain from his face with his scarf.

'What happened?'

'We engaged a large, mixed bag of Huns. There were some new ones I'd not seen before. A yellow-tailed Pfalz was close behind me. Peter dropped down between me and the Pfalz. I think the Hun's propeller cut into his tail.'

What an effort it was to climb from the cockpit.

'And what about Smith?'

He leaned against the fuselage for a moment. 'Smith rammed the Pfalz, maybe by accident, maybe not, I couldn't be sure. Anyway, he's dead too.'

Baker was running over to them, lurching clumsily in his heavy flying boots. 'Corby! I say, Corby. What are we going to do about that new feller, Elroy? We can't get him out of his cockpit. He's just sitting there, shaking like a leaf.'

Marten knew he must at least give the appearance of calm. He couldn't even remember who Elroy was. 'What's the matter with him?'

'God knows. He's sitting there grinding his teeth and

hanging onto the stick like grim death. I thought he looked scared before we took off, but I didn't realise he was that bad.'

What the hell did they expect him to do about it? But he and McGraw went. Then he recognised Elroy as the replacement who'd sung in the fine tenor voice, the night they'd heard Richthofen was dead. The night he'd drawn the line separating himself from Peter.

He and McGraw got either side of the cockpit to drag Elroy's hands off the control column and lift him out. Then they walked him, glassy-eyed and jaw clenched, to the sick quarters.

Thank God Kit Carson was due back from the hospital at Etaples. It would take the pair of them, and McGraw, the rest of the day to sort out what should be done.

'Captain Carson isn't coming back,' McGraw said. 'They've diagnosed TB. He's already on his way back to England.'

Pour it down, David, pour it down. My boots aren't full yet.

He and McGraw went to Peter's office and he sat himself wearily in Peter's old swivel chair. He must think. 'Tea, Corporal!'

An orderly came over from the sick quarters because the sergeant in charge wanted Mr Corby or Mr McGraw to tell him what he should do about Lieutenant Elroy. He'd given him a strong sedative but it wasn't working. Did he have permission to send the gentleman to the Base Hospital at Amiens?

McGraw was looking his age, gnawing at his grey moustache and rubbing his stubby fingers through his short hair. 'They really ought to give us a medical officer. We have nobody here capable of dealing with this sort of thing.'

Saying that didn't solve the problem. Even if they got

Elroy as far as Amiens there was no certainty that the hospital hadn't already been evacuated. The Huns were hurling high velocity shells into the city. Marten made a quick decision because it was easier than discussing the matter with McGraw.

'Send Mr Elroy to the hospital at Doullens. The Huns shouldn't get that far this week.'

McGraw frowned but didn't say anything. The orderly room corporal came in with two mugs of tea, then hovered, pretending not to listen, until McGraw waved to him to get out. Marten turned the swivel chair to face the blackboard indicating pilot availability. McGraw picked up a rag and deleted the names of Peter, Smith, Tanner and Jacobson. Then he frowned and rubbed out Elroy and Carson. 'How does that leave us?'

'We were already one short, so now we have twelve pilots and thirteen machines. What do we do?'

McGraw took a deep breath. 'First we'll have to contact Wing and tell them Major West is dead.'

Yes. He couldn't really believe it, but it was so. And Wing would have to be told.

McGraw was chewing his moustache again. 'And we'll have to tell them we're non-operational until we get a new CO and some replacements.'

Common sense decreed it. But he was reluctant to agree, though he didn't know quite why. He needed time to think. But there was no time.

'Who do we contact at Wing?'

'Major Stocks.' McGraw was frowning again. 'And look. You'd better let me handle this. I'm used to dealing with these people. I'll say it's my considered opinion that we must have a stand-down for a day or two.'

He wasn't prepared to let McGraw do that. McGraw wasn't a pilot. And McGraw didn't really know what they could or could not do.

'No. I'm the only flight commander left. I'll talk to Stocks.'

McGraw looked as if he was going to assert himself, puzzled, not quite able to grasp the sudden change in their circumstances, but still sure that the decision should be his. Then he shrugged, picked up the telephone, and handed it to him.

The voice at the other end of the line was cuttingly abrupt, concerned with pilot strength and machine availability. It was a slide-rule voice, intoning the logistical requirements of a pending counter-attack. The clipped comments were broken by intermittent crackling on the telephone line.

'You want me to go *where,* sir?' Marten pressed the ear piece against his ear to catch every word. For God's sake, what was he being asked to do? There was a final crackling on the line that could have been 'Good luck', and it went dead.

'What did he say?'

He put the telephone down slowly and rubbed his hand over the scars on his face. 'He said that now the Huns had taken Villers-Brettoneux they're poised for an assault on Amiens. And if Amiens falls they will roll us right back to the coast. So General Rawlinson has ordered that Villers-Bretonneux be retaken at all costs. A counter-attack is to be mounted within the next few hours. We have to support the infantry. I have to go to Amiens to meet a Major Lowry who is the liaison officer for the 13th Australian Brigade, and then I'm to go with him to attend a briefing at 3rd Army Corps Headquarters. I've got to be there at nineteen hundred hours. That's what? Seven o'clock. What's the time now?'

McGraw looked aghast. 'But didn't he understand that we have no commanding officer, and we are six pilots short?'

'Yes. He did understand that. There's nobody to replace Peter at such short notice. So I've been made acting CO.'

'But this is madness!' McGraw's voice rose. 'Phone him back, for God's sake, and tell him that we're in no position to support anybody.'

'No.' Marten shook his head.

There was no getting out of it. No playing with abstractions concerning responsibility. No heart-searching about what he might or might not owe to Jean. No taking refuge in being twice-wounded. The issue was now perfectly clear. The counter-attack had got to succeed, and they were part of it.

McGraw rubbed his hand through his hair. 'Look, Corby. I've been soldiering for years, and I tell you that you're making an appalling mistake. You're a junior officer. If anything goes wrong they may well blame you. Take my advice. Phone Stocks back. Say we've reviewed the situation here and what they ask is impossible.'

It did seem unreasonable, though not impossible. And in the past he would have been quick to give the same advice that McGraw was now giving. But he'd never been in command before. No, he'd always kept well clear of responsibility. Even today he'd hung back as long as he could before taking his flight into the battle. But now it was all different. He couldn't tell Stocks that they were unable to fly tomorrow, because they bloody well could. And he couldn't say that they had no leader, because good or bad, he was their leader.

He stood up. 'I'm going to the briefing, Mac. I've got to.'

McGraw stood looking at him for a moment, then shrugged hopelessly. 'What do you want me to do?'

He chewed his thumbnail. There were a lot of problems to sort out very quickly. The thing was to make tentative decisions which allowed him room for manoeuvre. 'Start checking on the weather. Get the technical sergeant major to work on the machines. I want twelve repaired and ready by first light tomorrow. See Price and get all the machines fully armed and bombs racked up. Make sure that nobody gets drunk while I'm gone. I want to see them all as soon as I get back.'

McGraw nodded and left.

As soon as the door closed and he was alone, Marten could feel his confidence slipping. McGraw didn't think he was up to it. If it had been Smith who'd survived, maybe McGraw wouldn't have been so quick to suggest that they stand down tomorrow.

But there was no time now to ponder on whether McGraw was right. He must take a good look at the map before he went to the briefing. The corporal came in again and handed him a letter. It was from Jean. He stuffed it into his pocket, unread.

The car was waiting for him, and he'd only just found time to change from his flying boots. The driver was clearly worried about the time, and immediately accelerated, out past the guard hut and onto the road running due south to Amiens. The hills to the left were tinged, briefly red, then darkness began to settle over the softly undulating countryside. A single star shone brightly in the east, where the steady thump of guns and occasional lurid flashes indicated the fighting. The Huns were much nearer now. The dark shape of Amiens lay ahead. He was going to be late.

'See if you can go a bit faster.'

'Yes, sir.'

Now, as they were entering the suburbs of the city, and the meeting with Lowry was almost upon him, doubts loomed large and McGraw's advice seemed irrefutable. Too late. He was committed.

The driver had slowed the car and was peering ahead into the darkened streets. The French Military Authority had ordered all the civilians to evacuate and Marten could see only a long column of soldiers on their way through. The sounds of their boots echoed hollowly off the empty houses on either side.

The driver detoured and came out near the grim Palais de Justice. There were dead horses on the steps, hurled up by an earlier explosion that had left a deep crater in the road. It was bloody criminal to treat horses this way. He could smell the poor beasts as the car inched its way round the shell hole.

The driver was detouring to avoid a slow-moving heavy artillery battery. They crossed the river by the stone bridge. The bombed railway station looked a mess. Most of the glass roof had fallen in. Now that the night had come they would be bringing the wounded back here, to move them west, to Abbeville or Etaples. The Anzac hospital had been nearby, but it was dark and empty now.

There was a crash and a tinkling of glass. Then the anti-aircraft guns all started firing at once. Marten craned his head out of the window of the car and looked up. The bloody Gothas were back. He could see them moving like bats across the moon.

At the Hotel St Roche the driver stopped and went inside to find Major Lowry. Down below, in the cellars, it was still possible for officers to get a candle-lit meal and a bottle of good wine.

Splinters from the anti-aircraft shells whistled down and cracked on the cobbles. A fire had started and he could hear the angry crackling of burning timber. The flames would show for miles, guiding in more bloody Gothas. Over the tops of the houses the pinnacles and buttresses of the cathedral reflected the deep red glow.

The driver reappeared with a tin-hatted officer.

'You're late. If you'd been on time we could have missed this air raid.'

A stick of bombs crashed down into the heart of the city. Lowry was ill at ease and began poking the driver in the back with his swagger stick. 'Go faster, man!'

Marten needed information. 'What about the counter-attack, sir?'

'Oh, that.' The major's voice was testy. He lit a cigarette with a practised flick of his lighter. 'Foch wants Villers-Bretonneux retaken, Rawlinson wants it retaken, so the Aussies are going to have a go. But I don't see it coming off. Recce party went in just before dusk. Cut to pieces.' He blew smoke out hurriedly as he spoke.

'Who is planning the counter-attack?'

'It's a 3rd Army Corps job, so I suppose Butler is organising it. We'll see when we get there.' Lowry, visibly relaxing now that the city was behind them, slumped down in his greatcoat.

'Have you any idea what the part of my squadron will be?'

Lowry shrugged impatiently. 'The whole thing was conceived this afternoon. I don't know anything about it. I merely report back to Wing with details of what the Aussies intend.' He sat in silence for a moment. 'Don't promise too much, that's all.'

The car swung off the road and stopped at wide gates. Provost men looked in and shone torches in their faces. Lowry held up a typed order and the torches went out.

'Straight ahead. You can't miss it.'

The driver accelerated along the driveway, and through gaps in the trees the huge château headquarters of the 3rd Army Corps reflected whitely the pale light of the moon. There were a dozen or more cars parked outside, among them a big Daimler with a Corps pennant on the bonnet.

What little confidence Marten had slid rapidly. What the hell would he say if they asked him questions? Clearly they would see that leading a flight of six machines was more than enough for him to cope with.

'You're late. The briefing has begun.' A very young, immaculately dressed colonel looked him up and down. 'God, you look a mess! But there's no time now to worry abut that.' He led them across a vast, candle-lit hall. It was damp and cold. The owners must have long since departed. There were shadows on the walls where pictures had been taken down.

They paused in front of an oak-panelled door, and Lowry whispered to him again, 'Remember, don't promise too much.' And they went in.

The room was lit by hurricane lamps, and some candles stuck in tins. Four brigadiers stood at the far side of a long table, glancing alternately at a large map spread before them, and a blackboard set obliquely at the table's end. Just inside the doorway a French colonel was talking softly to a young American officer who was nodding gravely. A dozen or more officers were standing in the shadows. The attention of the group was centred on a square-faced brigadier-general, talking rapidly with a broad Australian twang, and punctuating his comments with sweeping movements of his hands across the chalk-drawn map on the blackboard.

'The enemy has the whole of the town of Villers-Bretonneux, and the neighbouring high ground, stuffed with men and machine guns. Their 4th Guards Division is here. And their 77th Division, just back from Russia, is holding this area here. Down here, south of the town, is the 13th Division, mainly Westphalian troops.'

Yes, he could follow all that.

'Lieutenant-General Butler wanted us to attack at eight o'clock this evening, while there was still some light, but I strongly resisted this proposal. We go at ten tonight. And we are not going to attempt a frontal assault. We are going to move round the town and cut it off.'

Well, that at least was an improvement on sending the infantry over in waves, against machine guns.

'The 15th Brigade will attack from the north, down behind the town. We of the 13th Brigade will move south of the town. The 51st Battalion will lead and advance four thousand yards, then turn north to meet up with the 15th Brigade. Thus we will pincer the enemy positions. English battalions will then go in and mop up resistance in the town itself. Questions?'

'All this in darkness, sir?' The French colonel looked sceptical.

'Yes. It will be difficult, but it can be done.'

'And your preliminary bombardment, sir?'

'*No* preliminary bombardment. The whole success of this counter-attack depends on surprise. We want the Huns out of Villers-Bretonneux by tomorrow morning.'

It looked possible. Marten surprised himself by asking a question. 'Sir. Will the 13th and 15th Brigades have time to dig in before daylight? The enemy are bound to try and pierce your encircling ring.'

The brigadier-general stabbed a finger in his direction. 'Right. You're going to give us air support, aren't you?'

'Yes, sir.' He felt too involved now to care about the curious glances at his face, and his dirty leather coat.

'I'm counting on you. We want warning of enemy troops massing anywhere within three miles of our pincer. So you will have to patrol to the south and east of our positions. You'll alert us by firing orange flares immediately over any enemy build-up. Our artillery will shell the area you have indicated. Those first two hours of daylight will be critical.'

The brigadier-general smiled grimly. 'I don't have to

remind you all, gentlemen, that if we do not succeed, and the Germans get sufficient reinforcements into Villers-Bretonneux, their next stop will be Amiens. Maybe they won't even stop. Now I need to talk to my battalion commanders. We have a lot to do before ten. I don't need to keep the rest of you.'

As Marten and Lowry turned to leave, the brigadier-general called to him. 'Your best support, mind. And good luck.'

'You'll have it, sir,' he said. And he meant it, though God knows how he was going to do it with only twelve machines.

'I told you not to promise too much,' Lowry said as they got into the car.

He hadn't thought that he'd offered much.

Lowry was even more sceptical now. 'Attacking in the dark. No preliminary bombardment! Battles are not displays of virtuosity.'

Marten had too much on his mind to debate the matter. 'What sort of help can we expect from other squadrons in the area?'

'I might be able to get some F2b's, or some Camels from 209 Squadron to cover you. But they may already be committed elsewhere.' Lowry shrugged and stared out at the night. It didn't look as if he cared that much.

And so he returned to the squadron.

McGraw had them all waiting in the mess, and even called them to attention for God's sake. So he just waved them to sit down and began talking.

Harvey didn't bat an eyelid when he told him to lead a section of four planes and support the 15th Brigade north of the Amiens – St Quentin road. The southern end of the pincer he saved for his own section of three, because an attack was more likely there.

'So I'm to provide cover for you and Harvey with just

five machines,' Baker said. 'What do I do if Richthofen's Circus attacks? The baron may be dead but his hot-shot flyers are still in the area.'

'You hold them off for as long as you can. Major Lowry may get us some help, but we can't count on it. Two hours. I've promised them our strongest support for two hours.'

Baker looked bitter. 'I don't fancy getting buried, supporting a crazy plan like this.'

He wasn't going to discuss it. There was no time for cajoling, or jollying them along. 'We stay up there for two hours, or until we're all shot down. You'd better go and get some sleep.' He leaned back in his chair, weary beyond belief.

Now that deep night had come, and he was alone, the anxieties began to turn into a huge, crawling fear. And it was no good telling himself that in the morning the fear would become manageable again. There were things he must do. He would go over to Peter's office and work there until he was too tired to think any more.

It was well gone midnight. The whole camp was quiet. He could hear only the light pattering of rain on the window, and occasional noises of machinery in the workshops fifty yards away. Peter's in-tray was still half full; reports, memoranda, orders from Wing, just as he'd left it before he took off for his last patrol. In the drawer, behind the whisky bottle and glasses, there was a leather folder with a photograph of Mary. Tucked under the photograph was an envelope addressed in Mary's handwriting. From the date on the envelope he could guess that it was the final letter. He couldn't bring himself to read it, though what the hell difference did it make now? They had all done what they had done. This was no time to apportion blame. He would blame himself tomorrow perhaps. Right now he had to balance his load as best he could.

He took Jean's letter from his pocket and began to read it.

If it were not for the distant, muted sounds of the guns, he could almost imagine himself back in that other world. Jean had a new lab assistant so she didn't have to work quite so hard. He was very young and very poor. He flirted with her, made her tea, and borrowed his tram fare home every Thursday evening. The air raids had stopped, so he mustn't worry about her. Old Mr Solomons' other son, Maurice, had been invalided out of the army and now walked with a limp, but the old man was so pleased to have him home again and safe. The daffodils were out. She had been invited to tea with his father and mother, and his father had talked about him the whole time. Mrs Payne had begun to tend her window-box again, so maybe she was getting over Fred's death. Although the newspapers were reporting heavy fighting, they seemed to suggest that the Germans were being held. And now that the Americans had joined the Allies the war would surely end soon. He would come home and they would walk in the park. They would sit with the sun on their faces. And he would tell her about the ducks. She missed him. She missed him.

He might be able to sleep now, because he did suddenly feel very tired. He would rest his head on the desk for a moment.

Harvey was saying something to him. He stirred himself and stretched back in Peter's old swivel chair, stiff from sleeping with his head on his folded arms.

'Corby, are you all right? I got worried about you.'

'What time is it?'

'It's gone one o'clock. Listen, the gunfire has died down.'

'Why are you still awake?'

'Oh, things on my mind.'

'Like what?' But he couldn't stop yawning as he said it.

'They'll keep. Look, I found Smith's red silk scarf. That was the only time I ever remember him flying without it. He said it brought him luck. You'd better carry it tomorrow.'

'Right. And tell me what's worrying you.'

'I'll tell you tomorrow.'

'All right,' he said, because he couldn't think straight. Maybe he should have made an effort, but he really was too tired.

*

Fourteen

EVEN THOUGH it was still dark, the morning brought guarded confidence. And taking care over small things, like shaving, helped to dull the jagged edges of his doubts. He'd wear three pullovers today because it was going to be cold up there. Dragging on flying boots stiffened resolution, and Smith's red silk scarf around his neck was warm and oddly comforting.

The others would have confidence if he had, so he would walk purposefully into the mess. Was that why old Hook had always stumped about so?

But the atmosphere was tense as he opened the door and entered. They looked like condemned men hoping for a reprieve. St John was nervously waving away the orderly's tray.

'Come on, St John. Eat up your egg like a good boy.' Marten sat in Peter's chair at the head of the table.

Baker grimaced and poked at his egg with his spoon. 'They make me fart at six thousand feet. Something to do with the pressure.'

'Don't worry. The SE5 is a very robust machine. It will stand it.' He turned to the mess orderly. 'Give Mr Baker another boiled egg. He might manage to frighten off Richthofen's Circus.'

Could he detect a slight upturn in their spirits? He started to shovel down his egg, with assumed relish, Smith-like, though every mouthful was like chewing sawdust.

'But don't drink too much tea, Gates. We'll be in the air for two and a half hours, and you'll pee like a cart

216

horse when we get back.'

Somebody laughed. He must encourage the idea that they would return, to quite simple things.

Harvey said, 'now I know how my grandpa must have felt just before the Battle of Gettysburg.'

'How is the old fellow?'

'Still re-living the Civil War.'

'You'll do the same when you're old. You'll sit on the porch and tell your grandchildren how you helped stop General Ludendorff's March Offensive. Who knows, we might make history today.'

Harvey grinned wryly. 'You're not *just* an ugly face, Corby.'

Price had been up half the night with his armourers. 'Four bombs racked up on each machine. Every gun has been stripped and cleaned. Every cartridge has been smeared with oil. You shouldn't have any stoppages.'

The technical sergeant major, grey with fatigue, said that all twelve machines were ready. There was a bloodstained bandage on his thumb. It was odd because for the first time since Drinkwater's death, the sight of blood didn't disturb him.

McGraw had been on the telephone to 3rd Army Corps Headquarters. 'Amazing!' He chewed excitedly at his moustache. 'The fighting was very heavy, but the Australians have completely encircled the town. They're digging in all round the perimeter.'

'Then there's nothing to keep us here.' Marten pulled on his helmet.

The German pilots would be getting ready as well. And their infantry machine gunners would be pulling the sacking off their guns and peering round the dark sky, wailing for first light.

He walked across to the twelve machines, lined up, grey shapes against the dawn. The sky overhead was clear and a few bright stars lingered as the sun came up beyond the front.

Mechanics were busying themselves. The pilots stood in a small group, waiting for him.

'Is that Captain Smith's scarf you're wearing, sir?'

'Yes. A bit of Smith will bring us luck today.' He counted up quickly. Only Harvey had not yet joined them. St John was climbing into his cockpit.

'Hey! St John. Don't forget to allow for the weight of the bombs when you take off.'

St John nodded. He was probably too nervous to speak.

'Stick close to me. But not so close that you chew my wing off. And you, Gates, stay on my right.'

Time to go. Where was Harvey?

An engine coughed in the chill morning air, then burst into life with a deep, full-throated roar. Harvey was approaching with a swinging step, tightening the strap of his helmet as he walked. He had an envelope tucked under his belt.

'Harvey, are you all right?' Then he remembered. 'I didn't ask you what was worrying you last night.'

'I'm fine now.' Harvey paused. 'I've written a letter to my parents. You keep it for me, just in case.'

'Oh hell, Harvey!' Once you began to think about dying you were half done for. Another engine caught and fired. 'Give it to McGraw,' he shouted.

'No, I'd rather you kept it,' Harvey shouted back.

'All right. I'll take it.' He stuck it inside his leather coat. 'I'll give it back to you later.' There was only time now to grip Harvey's shoulder and call, 'Good luck!'

They flew in three small sections towards the rising sun. Now he could see colours as the greyness faded. Baker's five machines had begun to climb to provide them with cover. Below, the Ancre river curved away to Albert and the north. And there, on the high ground between the two rivers, Villers-Bretonneux stood strangely clear of smoke and gas.

Harvey's section had to break away to support the 15th Brigade. Marten waved to him, and Harvey raised his hand in a last salute then half-rolled off to the left followed by the rest of his section. No good to watch him. He must manage on his own.

He veered south with St John and Gates, over the stark, fretted ruins of the town. The three battalions of the 13th Brigade were spread out along a rim, joining up with the 15th Brigade in the north-east. Australian soldiers were waving up at them from their hastily-dug ditches. Mortar shells were thumping down on them from the German positions, still held in the town.

They had to go in low and find the Huns where they were thickest. At four hundred feet the ground fire was so intense that tracer trails criss-crossed all around them. A bullet smacked up through the side of the cockpit and knocked the goggles off his head. God's teeth! He was shaking with fear and shock. His heart thumped painfully. He must take a deep breath and grope for the spare goggles.

In Hangard Wood the Huns were massing for an assault on the Australian perimeter, so he flew low over the tightly-packed infantry. There were thousands of them down there. He fired off the first orange flare. St John and Gates followed him round as he swept back and released all his bombs, scattering the companies below him. Almost immediately Australian shells were smashing into the wood, shattering huge trees and ripping them out by their roots.

Gates still had his bombs. Excited, he must have forgotten to release them. Marten waved to him and pointed, but Gates shook his head, uncomprehending.

219

There was no time to signal again. They were back over the St Quentin road, banking through the white streaks of tracers.

Grey-clad infantry were spilling out from Warfusse; sections, platoons, companies, running from shell hole to shell hole towards the Australian rim. Marten signalled to the others and dived again, steering his stream of bullets into the largest groups. There was a dull thump on his right and black smoke and falling debris where Gates had been. Marten fired another orange flare, then climbed with St John to look down on the scene below. Shells began to fall among the German infantry. Whole companies were faltering, some even turned back, while others huddled deep in the shell holes. It was like being an Old Testament prophet, calling down fire on the small, sprawled figures, desperately covering their heads with their arms.

He peered around the sky. Baker's section was high above them. No enemy machines had appeared yet, but it wouldn't be long before they came. The Red Baron's Circus was at Cappy and they must surely be in the air by now. The sky was clear. Far off to the left he could see Harvey's small group, turning amidst the shell bursts.

He changed the drum on the Lewis gun and turned to St John to wave. Just the two of them now and they needed mutual encouragement. But St John was pointing up to a descending trail of smoke. Baker's worst fears were now realised. Dozens of brightly-coloured shapes, deceptively like toys, were wheeling above them, then rolling to right and left, diving down on them. Time only to kick the rudder hard and skid sideways as some of them dropped through Baker's scattered machines and down on him and St John. Now he must use every skill, snap roll to the right, fire, level out, push the stick forward and kick right rudder, dive and zoom up again. St John was above him, swinging from side to side with a garish triplane on his tail. Climb up, fire again. No time to watch as the triplane crumpled and fluttered down.

The coloured machines were all around them. Skid right, kick the rudder, skid left. A dirty brown trail was gushing from St John's engine as he dropped earthwards. This was the end then. Take on the scarlet machine and ram it head on rather than give way. He'd go down like Smith, and join Peter and the Killer in the Great Beyond. The Hun pulled his nose up at the last minute, exposing his belly, and he raked it from end to end.

But for God's sake what had happened? Had he chased them all off on his own? The Huns were scattering to the east, small already against the sun. Big brown two-seaters had appeared from nowhere and were fast after them. Dear God, bless Lowry for keeping his casual word. He'd build a shrine to him. He'd petition the Pope to have Lowry canonised. A last skirmish as three triplanes fired hasty bursts at the pursuing F2b's then vanished.

The sky was suddenly quiet. He was alone, flying straight and level in the still air.

He'd have to pull himself together and take a deep breath. Then he'd have to find the others because they'd be waiting for him to lead them home. As he pushed the stick hard over and extended his leg against the rudder bar, he felt a stabbing pain that made him gasp. Funny that he hadn't noticed it before. It was as if a dog had sunk his teeth deeply into his left calf. Even when he eased his foot on the bar the pain was still there and the leg felt weak and ineffective. It must be bleeding because the leg was wet inside his boot. But he could still work the rudder by pressing and pulling with his right foot inside the stirrup.

Low over the Somme, near Vaux, the three remaining members of Baker's section had gathered, flying in lazy circles while he approached. Baker wasn't with them.

The Australians of the 3rd Division were waving, faces turned up, mouths open as if they were cheering.

Had Harvey and his three all gone? Bank and circle once more, and wait.

The sky was very blue, with traces of icy cirrus high up. And to the west small clumps of cumulus clouds drifted slowly. Dear God, don't let Harvey be dead too.

Three machines were approaching, climbing rapidly to join them. Powell, Hutchens, and yes, Harvey! The three circled. Marten could see Harvey's white teeth bared in a grin.

He heaved a huge sigh. They'd done it. The F2b's could look after things now. The Australians would be well dug in around their perimeter, and the English battalions would be clearing Villers-Bretonneux. Amiens was safe, for a while, maybe for good. And maybe this really was the turning point that Peter had talked about.

The pain in his leg was easing now that he wasn't using it. He pulled off his glove and slid his hand down the back of his boot. The bottom part of his calf was numb to the touch and sticky with blood. So he wouldn't be flying again for a while.

It was like a lifetime since yesterday. Peter wouldn't have to worry any more; destiny had caught up with him. They would have buried what was left of him on that high ground, between the Somme and the Ancre, where Richthofen had gone down, and Smith, and Yellow Tail, and all those others whose names he couldn't even remember.

And it was no good his crying like this, tears would only steam up his goggles. He pulled them up and tilted his face towards the lashing stripstream, taking huge gulps of air.

He let the plane fly itself. The compass needle drifted slightly and he corrected his direction with a very slight pull on the stirrup of the rudder bar. The compass needle moved back to two-eight-zero and steadied.

The others were spread out in a ragged V behind him, and at each small movement that he made, they adjusted to him, as if the controls under his hands and feet extended to them. Harvey looked across at him and raised his hand. He waved back, then took Harvey's letter from under his coat and tore it into shreds, the bits of paper fluttering back behind him. Harvey was smiling.

Soon Harvey's countrymen would finish the war. One day generals, and scholars in quiet universities would write books about what should have been done and what lessons had been learned. But the good men who'd fought and died here will care little what they say.

He pulled the goggles down over his eyes again and tightened Smith's scarf around his neck. And he suddenly remembered: it was his birthday. Today he was twenty-one.

For him the game was over; he knew it now with absolute certainty. He was going home to marry Jean. And spring was here. You could tell by the fading browns and bright greens below. He and Jean would walk in the park. And they'd sit near the pond's edge and watch the birds swooping low over the water.